THE TWO-WEEK ARRANGEMENT

New York Times & USA Today Bestselling Author

KENDALL RYAN

ABOUT THE BOOK

Dear Sexy AF Intern,

I know you don't particularly care that I'm the CEO of this company, and you're just an intern. I also know you're not impressed by my power or my wealth, and that's fine.

You think you've got me all figured out from working alongside me for two weeks, but you don't know me. Not really.

You don't know that I'm a single dad to twin toddlers, or that those two little girls matter more to me than this entire hotel chain.

I'm not interested in starting something deep and meaningful, but what I am interested in is the way your body reacts to mine when we're in the same room. You probably assume the concentration on my face is work-related, when in reality, I'm figuring out which I want more—to nail you against the wall or bend you over my desk.

While you're too disciplined to act on it, I'm not. And the night you stepped into my limo, all bets were off.

PROLOGUE

Presley

I have fourteen days to win the job of my dreams. Two weeks of working alongside billionaire hotelier Dominic Aspen to land an executive spot at the most prestigious hotel chain in the world.

There's just one thing standing in my way: one six-foot-two, infuriatingly sexy thing, my new boss—Dominic Aspen.

If the rumors swirling about him are true, I have no idea how I'll make it through this in one piece. He's intense, demanding, and mysterious.

But I need this job more than you can imagine.

I won't play games, won't fall for his charms.

Too bad Dominic doesn't play fair. In fact, I'm not certain we're playing the same game.

One touch, and I'm putty in his hands. One whispered promise, and I'm done for.

But I was never supposed to fall in love . . .

CHAPTER ONE

Dominic

"Been out with anyone lately?"

The tension headache that's been threatening all day finally sets in, throbbing low in the base of my skull. I shake my head at Oliver's ridiculous question, my gaze not straying from the screen of my laptop.

"You know I don't have time to date," I say, more than a little exasperated that we've had this conversation approximately six thousand times.

Just because Oliver is in a happy relationship doesn't mean he needs to force monogamy down everyone else's throats. I'm perfectly happy being single.

"Come on, man. You without pussy is like macaroni without cheese."

My vice president, ladies and gentlemen.

"Fuck's sake, Ollie. Do you have to be so crass?"

This recurring conversation is wearing thin. I'm about three seconds away from kicking him out of my office. Or kicking him in the nuts. Whichever comes first. Maybe I'll kick him in the nuts and then kick him out. It's not like he doesn't deserve both.

Oliver only scoffs as he wanders to the far end of the office and reaches for a cut-crystal glass from the bar cart. The glass decanters hold fine aged Scotch and the best gin money can buy, but I rarely touch the stuff. It's there for two purposes—on the rare occasions when I'm entertaining clients, and for Oliver. The man drinks like a fish, though he rarely lets himself get intoxicated by some miracle of his metabolism. But I take no issue with it. It's well after six, and technically speaking, our work-day is over.

Without bothering to ask me if I'd like a glass, he simply pours himself two fingers of Scotch and then joins me again, sinking into the plush black leather wingback across from my desk. He only takes one sip before continuing the criticism.

"Don't be such a priss, Dom." He pauses to look at me, his eyebrows raised in amusement as if he's about to let me in on an inside joke. "You must have forgotten."

I lean forward and place my elbows on the desk. "Forgotten what?"

He smirks, swirling the liquor in his glass. "That I know all of your quirks."

I roll my eyes. That's a polite way of putting it. At least he didn't call it a sexual deviance again. The memory of *that* conversation last month makes me shudder.

It's true that Oliver knows me well. I'd be the first to admit my best friend and vice president has gotten me out of some unseemly situations over the years, but that doesn't mean I want to discuss my sex life with him.

Even though we've been friends since we grad-uated from Princeton, there are certain boundaries I like to maintain now that I'm his boss. In some ways, those years seem like only yesterday, and in others, they feel like a lifetime ago. Even if Oliver hasn't changed much, I feel like a completely different person.

"You know the only two ladies I have time for are Emilia and Lacey."

Defeated, he sighs. "Yeah, yeah. I know."

I would appreciate it if Oliver didn't always forget the two little girls waiting at home for me to read them bedtime stories and check for monsters under the bed. Children certainly aren't on Oliver and Jessica's radar at this point in their relationship.

They weren't on mine, either.

"Besides, there will be time for fun and games later. The internship program begins Monday." I skim over the schedule my assistant has compiled for me.

Oliver drums his fingers on the arm of his chair. "Damn, that's right."

A handful of the best and brightest recent college graduates from all over the nation were selected out of more than a thousand applicants to join Aspen Hotels on a trial basis. For the next two weeks, they will be responsible for learning our current business model and executing the forward motion of our hotels into a more modern format.

It's not the first time Aspen has offered this internship, but it may be the last. Outreach initiatives like this have proven successful from the public relations standpoint, but employee retention from these internships has never impressed me. I guess that's the one thing I inherited from my father, the late Phillip Aspen—perpetually low expectations.

"Since when did we believe in internships?" Oliver grumbles into his drink.

Once again, he's read my mind. Despite my misgivings about the program's success, I do need a new director of operations. Desperately. This internship, with some tweaks, will help me find a candidate who's fresh and hungry, not someone so set in their ways that they refuse to do things my way.

"We need to reevaluate our operations if we're going to survive in this market. Internships are an excellent way of bringing in new blood without losing money on new hires who prove to be financial risks."

"That was pointed." Oliver laughs.

"Terry wasn't a new hire. Terry was a very old hire who needed a wake-up call."

"I was talking about Kylie."

"Oh." Kylie was briefly our director of operations, after Terry's resignation.

"Why did we fire her, anyway?"

"She had some unreasonable expectations."

Oliver raises his brows in question, but he knows better than to ask.

I don't condone unwarranted sexual advances from my employees at our philanthropic events, no matter the blood-alcohol content. I also don't ruin a perfectly capable woman's career by broadcasting her actions to my friends and coworkers after she throws herself at me. Instead, I quietly fire her with a sizable severance package and an emphatic *good riddance.*

"So that's what you're trying to get out of this? A new director of operations? Look, Dom, I respect your choices, and God knows, I let you make most of them. But recent college graduates don't necessarily have the experience we need at the helm of our entire operation."

I smirk. "I'm glad my father didn't feel that way when he hired you as a consultant fresh out of college."

Oliver raises his hands in surrender. "Point taken. And I'm glad you decided you needed a vice president to help you run this shit show."

He lifts his glass in a friendly toast. I mime the gesture in return.

Ping.

An email grabs my attention. It's our marketing director, proposing the updated social media branding for my approval. I examine it with a critical eye—each and every font, each pigment of color. It's classic, but still somehow fresh, and doesn't stray from our brand. I decide that I like it, and shoot off an email telling her as much.

"Do you ever stop working?" Oliver is leaning so far back into the chair that I have to look over my screen to make eye contact.

"Nope. Shouldn't you be headed home soon to Jess?"

"She's off on business." He sighs, genuinely upset by her absence.

I smile. True love isn't all it's cracked up to be. Oliver and Jess are a thriving couple to all inquiring eyes. But as their friend, I know exactly how deep their codependence goes. I can tell that as soon as Oliver leaves my office, he'll be on the phone with her, asking about her day.

He's fucking whipped.

"Well, chin up, brother. Tomorrow should be interesting, right?"

"For you, maybe." Oliver frowns. "I don't have the luxury or energy to enjoy the company of young *attractivos*."

I smile at Oliver's choice of words. He hasn't lost any of his quirks since settling down. If anything, his propensity for made-up words has only been encouraged by his other half.

"You should enjoy the next two weeks, though." Oliver tips his glass toward me.

"How so?"

"Get yourself some new blood." He gives me a

devilish grin.

Ah, yes. Back to square one. How do we always end up here? Oh, right, because Oliver has a one-track mind.

"Aspen Hotels needs new blood. Dominic Aspen is just fine," I respond firmly.

"When's the last time you had a woman in your bed?" he asks.

I don't indulge him with an answer, mostly because I can't remember, but also because it's none of his damn business.

"That's what I thought." Oliver grins, knowingly. "And when's the last time you had a conversation with a woman that you weren't paying?"

"Are we done with this lecture yet? I have work to do," I grumble.

Oliver doesn't respond, only slides out of the chair and places his glass on my desk, temptingly close to my hand. "Good night, Dom."

"Good night, Oliver." He has his phone in his hand, dialing Jess before he's even out the door.

Classic.

I run my hand through my hair and eye the clock on the far wall. Past dinnertime. I don't have much of an appetite, but I know I should eat. I should also go home early for once, relieve the nanny, and see my beautiful daughters before they're tucked away in bed.

Yet, here I sit. Staring at the drops of Scotch at the bottom of someone else's glass.

Dominic Aspen is just fine.

CHAPTER TWO

Presley

Y*ou're only as small as your dreams.*

That's what my mother said to me in the hours before cancer took her. That sentiment is the cornerstone I've based my life on ever since. I don't do small. It's not in my vocabulary. I dream big or not at all. I take risks, fight for what I want, and push myself to live life to the fullest.

It's the only way I know how to honor my mother's words. I also make sure my younger brother does the same. He's just finished his first year at one of the country's most prestigious ballet academies.

My mother would be proud of us both. My father, not so much. She would hate the man he's become.

He never calls, and when we do talk, he speaks mostly in grunts and monosyllables. He's about as supportive as an overcooked noodle. He threatened to back out of paying for my brother's schooling if he majored in dance, and then made good on that promise when Michael came out as gay.

But I swore to Michael that we don't need him, our father who I now view as little more than a sperm donor. Sure, I'll have to work a little harder, dream a little bigger, to take care of both my brother and myself, but it's nothing I can't do.

Which leads me to today.

"Today's the day, huh?" my best friend and roommate, Bianca, asks from her perch on the couch.

I gulp down one last sip of my now cold coffee and grimace as I swallow. "Yup. Today's the day."

"You're not nervous, are you?" She levels me with a deadpan stare. "You're the baddest bitch I know, Presley."

I chuckle and roll my eyes. Bianca is good for my ego. Every time I brought home a paper with an A, every report card that boasted a perfect 4.0 grade point average, every scholarship I was awarded and internship I succeeded at, Bianca would only give me a knowing stare. It was her equivalent of saying *see, I told you so.*

But this internship is different. She knows that as well as I do. Rather than taking the safety net of a steady job when we graduated last month, I held out hope that I would win one of the coveted spots at Aspen Hotels.

And now that I have, the butterflies inside my stomach are kicking around like crazed ninjas.

At my pause, she rises and grips my shoulders, giving them a comforting squeeze. "Tell me you're not worried."

"About the internship? No."

But I'm lying. I am a teensy bit worried. It's only human, right? This is the biggest opportunity I've ever had, and I don't want to blow it. And there's the not-so-little issue of money. The internship is unpaid.

I let out a slow exhale. "It's just . . . what the heck am I going to do for money, B?"

I've just signed on for three months of unpaid

work in the hopes of landing my dream job. But hope doesn't pay the bills. I do. Or rather, I *did*.

Bianca doesn't try to sugarcoat things or blow off my concern as something trivial. She knows me well enough to know I wouldn't be stressed unless there was truly something to worry about. And she knows the tuition at my brother's school is astronomical.

She just scratches her chin, looking concerned. Trying to assure me, she says, "It'll all be fine."

I nod in agreement, but the truth is, she can't know that. I'm already behind on all my bills, and I've been supporting Michael since my dad disowned him last year. Knowing I've just agreed to take an unpaid internship doesn't exactly sit well with me. If I don't land the executive position at the end of this highly competitive internship, I'll be truly screwed.

Four of the country's top college graduates were accepted into the accelerated program, but I need to be the one to rise to the top—no ifs, ands, or buts about it.

Bianca fidgets. "You can stay here as long as you need to."

I nod at her offer, but the truth is I disagree. I don't want to overstay my welcome or take advantage of my best friend. Plus, crashing on her couch isn't exactly how I pictured living my best life post-graduation. I'm in my twenties now. It's time to get my shit together.

"I need to finish getting ready," I say to Bianca as I carry my mug to the sink and rinse it out.

"Knock 'em dead, girlfriend," she calls.

I head into the bathroom and grab a tube of lipstick from inside my makeup bag.

It only takes eight seconds to make a lasting first impression. These are the words I repeat to myself as I look in the mirror, fussing with my long, wavy brown hair. I arrange the dark tresses over one shoulder and purse my lips at my reflection.

I hate that I look younger than my twenty-two years. My friends tease that it will become an advantage later in life, but for now, having a baby face is annoying, to say the least. Especially when I want nothing more than to be seen as a professional businesswoman.

Actually, scratch that. I want to be seen as a confident business mogul. That's what it will take to win the job of my dreams. Coming across as flaky or too young will only hurt my chances.

For the next three months, I'll be competing for an executive position at the most prestigious hotel chain in the world. Working at Aspen Hotels has been my dream job forever. You don't grow up in Seattle and not know the Aspen brand. It's a coveted spot, and one I'll have to work hard for.

Drawing in a deep breath, I give myself a silent pep talk. *You've got this, Presley.* My inner voice sounds a lot like my mother, and that makes me break into a smile. Honoring her memory by busting my ass is pretty much my only pastime these days.

Despite my nerves, I know I'm ready for this. Dressed in a pair of black pants, a crisp white button-down shirt, and a pair of black heels, I'm ready for anything they throw my way.

Bring it.

• • •

The gleaming glass doors leading to the beautiful Aspen hotel have always been out of reach. But not today. I've never even been inside the lobby of a five-star hotel, but this morning, I stroll inside with purpose, pausing only briefly as my heels click across the shiny marble floors. The emailed instructions I received directed me to the nineteenth floor, so I proceed to the bank of elevators lining the far wall.

Everywhere I look there are fine tapestries and gleaming mahogany, elegant paintings, and helpful members of the hotel staff dressed in crisp navy-blue suits. I take in every detail surrounding me and can't help but smile as I step inside the elevator. On the nineteenth floor, I step out onto plush navy carpeting that contrasts with walls wallpapered in shades of cream.

A little-known fact about the hotel, at least this particular location in the heart of downtown, is that in addition to the six hundred guest rooms, it also houses the corporate offices, which are directly below the penthouse home of CEO Dominic Aspen.

His reputation as a CEO is that he's intense and demanding, and a little bit mysterious. I guess I'll find out.

I make my way to a meeting room at the far end of the hall. Before I enter, I check my phone and see that I'm eight minutes early. Perfect. I've always subscribed to the notion that on time is late, and early is on time.

When I enter, I'm greeted by a woman who looks to be in her fifties. She's short and stocky and has a ready smile when she spots me.

"Hello. Welcome. You must be Presley Harper." She holds out her hand in greeting, and I shake it.

"Yes, it's nice to meet you . . ."

"Beth Darvill, but Beth is fine. I'm the executive assistant to Mr. Aspen and the coordinator for the intern program. Please have a seat. We'll begin once everyone has arrived."

I settle into my seat at the large conference table and take stock of my competition.

A petite Asian girl sits beside me in an expensive-looking black suit, and a guy who looks to be of Indian heritage sits beside her with a serious expression. Neither greets me. We wait in silence for the fourth and final intern to arrive. With one minute to spare, he finally bursts into the room wearing a lopsided grin.

"I'm here! Made it in the nick of time. Jordan Provost."

As Beth gestures him into the seat beside me, I quickly take his measure. His tie is too loose and his hair is a little too long on the top. He reminds me of the frat guys I used to avoid during undergrad. *Fantastic.*

We spend the next hour receiving an overview of the internship program from Beth, and I also meet my fellow interns. In addition to Jordan, there's Jenny and Aarav. Apparently, the four of us have been selected from a pool of over a thousand applicants. I'm fairly certain that Jordan, with his tattered notebook and no pen to take notes with, is the son of someone important. Jenny, Aarav, and I all take dutiful notes on our laptops. I type every word Beth says just so I don't miss anything.

I learn that we'll share an open work space on the twentieth floor. That despite this internship being non-paid, we'll have access to the employee cafeteria, as well as the hotel fitness facility and pool.

I doubt I'll have much free time to go for a swim—I've heard to expect ninety-hour work weeks for the next three months, assuming I'll be the one chosen for this position—but that doesn't bother me. I'm here for one thing and one thing only. And I intend to win.

Beth pauses, and I lift my gaze to the front of the room. "You've each been paired with a member of our executive team. This person will act as a mentor to you and will oversee your day-to-day work on the project that you'll be assigned. You will have two weeks to make a great impression. If after those two weeks, you don't convince your mentor that you deserve a shot, you'll be let go."

A hushed silence falls over the room. I didn't know about this two-week stipulation, and it seems the other interns didn't either. This ups the ante even more.

Then Beth continues. "At the end of the three-month internship, the executive team will meet and discuss which of the remaining candidates they would like to extend an offer to. God willing, one of you will become a new *associate executive* here at Aspen Hotels."

I smile, giddy at the thought of the title associate executive behind my name.

"Now, let's take a short bathroom break, and I'll call the executive team in so that you can meet your mentor and get started on your assigned project." Beth rises to her feet in sensible pumps.

I scurry off to the restrooms at the end of the hall and quickly check my reflection and wash my hands. My bladder is too nervous for me to do anything else, so I head back to the conference room and find four new people already inside.

I slide into my seat and feel four sets of eyeballs appraising me. It's a little intimidating to know that these people probably know just about everything there is to know about me and I'm virtually flying blind here.

Actually, they've only spent time getting to know me on paper. They might know I had a full-ride academic scholarship to Brown, and that I graduated at the top of my class while working two jobs, but they don't know *me*. Not really. I pull a much needed deep breath into my lungs.

I recognize the man standing at the center of the room as Dominic Aspen, but wow is all my brain can come up with. Seeing him in person is so much different than reading about him in a business journal or seeing his photo online. He's well over six feet tall with broad shoulders that fill out his suit jacket perfectly and a trim waist, but it's not just his physical presence that overwhelms my senses, it's the amount of confidence he exudes. Dear God, he could bottle the stuff and sell it. He'd make a fortune. Maybe it's because his dark hair is perfectly styled, and there's an appraising gleam in his eyes, like he knows something we don't. Or maybe it's because I can't help but picture how his inky hair would look rumpled after sex. Either way, it tugs at something in me, and I can't take my eyes away from him as he speaks. His jaw is square and shaved close, and his lips are full and soft looking. In his hands are two things—a smartphone and a small leather case.

The way the tailored black suit stretches over his muscular chest and wide shoulders is distracting, to say the least, and I can't help my gaze from roaming, taking stock of him. But the guy's a twenty-six-year-old billionaire. I'm sure he can afford the best personal trainer, tailor, and nutritionist money can buy. But you can't buy confidence, and this guy has it in spades.

I think back to this morning at the apartment when I told myself I was ready for anything. Apparently, *anything* didn't include the heart-racing near panic attack I have when Dominic Aspen opens his mouth to speak, welcoming us personally to the company. And I definitely wasn't ready for my panties to become soaking wet when he fixes me with that heavy, dark blue stare of his.

What the hell? I take a deep breath and appraise his companions in an attempt to distract myself from his raw masculinity and my body's unwelcome reaction to it. His lips part, then come together again.

Two women flank his sides, both the very picture of professionalism. One is an older blonde wearing a gray suit, her hair in a tidy bun, and the other is a brunette who looks to be in her mid-thirties in a knee-length black dress. Neither offers any sort of smile.

The man at the end is the only one of the group smiling. His dimpled grin is almost infectious. He's tall, but not as tall as Dominic.

I suddenly feel foolish for not researching the executive staff more thoroughly online. I should know who they are, where they studied, their pet peeves. Everything. Then again, I had no idea I'd be paired to work with someone so important and vital to the company. I assumed that as an unpaid intern, I'd be assisting some low-paid grunt worker. But I guess it goes to show they really are taking this internship seriously.

I have no idea who my mentor may be, but I can't wait to find out. Then I realize that if Mr. Aspen himself is here, does that mean he's one of the mentors?

That can't be fair, can it? The intern who has direct access to the CEO would surely be at an advantage. Unless Dominic Aspen was direct witness to a screwup, and then you'd be out of here on the first elevator down. So maybe it's not an advantage after all.

Beth smiles warmly at Mr. Aspen before she starts again. "Wonderful. Now that we've discussed our expectations of you, I'd like to introduce you to your mentor for the next three months. Jenny, you'll be working with Pamela Brightworth."

The older blonde woman smiles and comes forward to shake Jenny's hand.

"Aarav, you've been paired with Renee Hildreth."

The brunette crosses the room and gives Aarav's hand a firm shake. "Go, Blue," she says to him, and Aarav smiles. They must share the same alma mater.

"Presley," Beth says, and then Dominic places his hand on her forearm to stop her. He leans close and whispers something to her in a hushed tone. Her eyes meet mine and she nods, whispering something to him in response.

"Presley, you'll be paired with Dominic," she says.

My stomach jumps.

I feel all the other interns eyeing me as this little announcement is made, and I can't help but wonder if they'll judge me, or think I'll have an unfair advantage being matched with the CEO himself.

Nerves twist inside me as Dominic approaches, pocketing his smartphone. He extends one large hand toward me, and I reach out to accept his greeting. The moment my hand is enclosed in his, chills skitter down my spine.

"It's nice to meet you," he says.

When his deep voice washes over me, I open my mouth to respond, but nothing comes out. Thankfully, Beth continues without missing a beat.

I don't even hear the remaining introductions, but Jordan is paired with the man—Oliver something, I think she says. It's impossible to hear much or to think clearly when my heart is thumping so hard that blood is roaring through my eardrums.

When everyone stands and begins to file out of the room, I rise to my feet, determined to put my momentary lapse in judgment behind me.

He's just a man, a very attractive man who runs a very big company. But at the end of the day, he puts his pants on one leg at a time, just like everyone else.

Maybe it wasn't the smartest idea to picture Dominic without pants, because suddenly he's standing in front of me and my cheeks are flaming.

"Dominic Aspen. It's nice to meet you." He extends his hand toward me, and I take it, shaking it firmly twice.

"I'm Presley Harper. I'm happy to be here."

"Are you ready? I'll show you to your work space." His voice is so deep and rich, little goose bumps break out over my arms.

I nod. "Let's do it." *Oh my God, did that sound sexual?* "I didn't mean do it. I just meant, yes, let's go upstairs. Not to your place or anything." I stammer, sure that my face is as red as a tomato.

Seeming amused by me and my obvious lack of a filter, Dominic only smiles. "This way."

Rather than wait for the elevator with the others, Dominic turns left out of the conference room and we duck into a stairwell that requires a special keycard to access.

We head up one flight of stairs and then enter what appears to be an office area, complete with rows of tidy gray cubicles, a wall of copy machines and printers, and a cluster of offices tucked into corners and lining the far wall. I get the sense that I'm looking at my new home away from home, and I like it. There's a serious, yet professional vibe in the air around us as the support staff busily tap away at keyboards in front of them.

"This will be your desk," Dominic says, stopping beside a small gray cubicle in the center of the room.

This is it, my home away from home for the next three months. I take a deep breath and nod. "Great. I'm ready to get started."

Dominic watches me with curiosity, a smirk tugging up his lips while my heart continues hammering away.

CHAPTER THREE

Dominic

Not all of her hair fits into the thin band tying up Presley's ponytail. A few pieces have escaped, framing her face. I can tell she'd rather it all fit neatly back by the way she efficiently tucks the strands behind her ears. She has delicate features, and her petite frame sits perched on the chair just outside my office. It's a little more distracting than I realized it would be.

After I left her to review our business history, she pulled her hair back and dug straight in, a look of concentration on her face.

I emailed her the necessary files for her perusal—who we deal with, how our staff is organized, which department handles which process, all the basics. There's no better way for her to learn than to read, and I have too many emails in my in-box to walk her through it all. She doesn't seem like the type who needs hand-holding anyway.

Even from across the office, I can see her brow furrowed in deep concentration. I realize I haven't read a single email since I sent her the files. I've been too preoccupied with staring at my newest hire.

Goddamn.

Presley really does look young. She can't be much older than legal drinking age. I pull up her résumé on my computer and skim over it for the second time today.

Brown graduate. *A rival.* I smirk.

GPA of 4.0. *To be expected.*

Won a national coding competition. *Interesting.*

She's impressive, to say the least, but not any more so than the other three candidates. Then, why was it that as soon as she walked in the room, I wanted her as my personal intern?

I swallow the obvious answer with a sip of

scalding coffee. *I'm attracted to her.*

Perhaps appointing her as my personal intern wasn't the wisest idea. It's obvious that my dick was making the executive decisions this time. I can't afford distractions. Then I realize it's not too late to change my mind.

I begin drafting an email to Beth.

Beth –

Please reassign Presley until further notice. Not the right fit. Perhaps trade with Oliver?

Dom

"I'm done."

Before I can click send, Presley is standing in my doorway, waiting for my response.

She's done? "Already?"

"Yes."

That's hard to believe. I gave her dozens of files containing documents of thirty or more pages each.

I close out of the email without sending it as she walks closer. "How could you get through those so quickly?"

"I reached out to Beth last week and asked for any learning materials. She shared all the ones that aren't your private office affairs with me. I was able to get through the confidential documents in an hour. I figure my time here shouldn't be spent learning how to spend my time here. I'd rather be of use to you."

Wow.

"I'm impressed," I say with a genuine smile. *Is that a blush I see on her cheeks?*

"It's basic preparatory work. Where should we begin?"

In moments, Presley is standing over my shoulder as I show her the online database she'll be using to access our business files. I explain to her our current hotel operations across the nation, not worrying about simplifying any language. She asks the right questions and admits when she'd like a recap on a particular subject. By the end, she offers to compile a spreadsheet of our favorite food and beverage vendors to compare prices. I'm sold.

"I'll just need to track down the account numbers so I can make the inquiries and get you some quotes. I should have it done in the next forty-eight hours."

"This would have been done already, but our last director of operations had a sudden exit from the company—" I stop short. *No need to explain yourself to a twenty-two-year-old intern.*

"Understandable. It's no trouble," she says.

Presley hasn't cracked a smile this entire conversation. I find myself wondering what her face would look like with those full pink lips curled up. I've seen her cheeks go rosy more than once now. What will it take to make her smile?

When she leans over my desk to pick up a folder with her name on it, I'm struck by the scent of her shampoo, vanilla and almond. It's classic, simple, understated. Just like her.

Fuck. Get it together, Dom. I take a sobering breath.

I've kept my entire personal life hidden from the public—my clients, employees, and the press. I can certainly keep my attraction to one woman in check. And I won't be trading her with Oliver on the basis of my horniness. Discriminating against someone in the workplace based on their looks isn't a practice I support. Even if her looks are wildly distracting. She's obviously more than qualified.

"Dominic?"

My eyes snap up to hers. *Shit.* "What did you say?"

"I asked if this is my first assignment." She's holding the folder that bears her name.

"It is." Inside the folder is my proposal for a new construction staffing dispersal. More people on neglected floors, less wasted energy on the floors that just need remodeling. It'll be a large expense, but worthwhile in the long run.

"When can we discuss it?"

"It's all in there."

"I believe that, but—apprentice to mentor— I'd like to spend a little time together," she says, and her face flushes. "To discuss the p-proposal. Of course."

"Sure," I say, fighting a smile. What is with this woman and her odd way of saying things? Her repeated use of sexual innuendo is apparently unintentional, which makes it all the more amusing.

"Five minutes of your time tomorrow, then? Unless you can go longer."

"I can go for as long as you'd like," I reply smoothly.

The tomato color flooding to her cheeks is immediate. *I can still tease, right?*

"Great." And just like that, she's off to her desk and I'm alone again.

I don't realize how much fun I've been having until Presley is out of sight.

I don't usually let my guard down with women. Any therapist would have a field day dissecting that one, but to me, it's pretty straightforward.

My train wreck of a relationship with Emilia and Lacey's mother made it incredibly difficult to trust anyone. I recall how I felt when she first told me she was pregnant. I experienced a euphoric sensation of flying when she said they were twin girls, followed by a swift, gut-churning swoop of falling when she said she wasn't going to keep them. I had no family left, and she was going to take away the only chance I'd have?

In all my life, I had never begged anyone before that moment. It was her choice, she insisted, which I couldn't argue with. But I could offer her a deal.

I would fund her travels to Prague and the other hidden gems of the world she longed to discover, and she would carry my daughters. I would give her everything she ever wanted from life—a world of adventure and spontaneity. And in return, I, and my unborn daughters, would stay out of it. Within the week, the papers were signed, and custody of Emilia and Lacey was all mine. Within months, I had twin daughters, and their mother was never to be seen again.

The coffee in my mug has gone cold. How long have I been sitting here, dredging up the past? And all because of what, my attraction to some twenty-two-year-old?

It occurs to me that that was our age when Sara and I first met. That's right. It's muscle memory. My body is simply remembering what I felt like as a horny twenty-two-year-old. Maybe Oliver was right, and I'm overdue for some female company. But that can be easily remedied.

An email pops up on my screen, a short reminder from Beth that I have a business dinner tomorrow night. He's an important client and potential investor in Aspen Hotels. *Perfect.*

Oliver loves to give me a hard time about paying for sex. He can never understand why I can't just pick up a woman at a bar, like any other bachelor our age. The truth is that I can. That's easy enough. But it's not the sex I'm paying for. I'm paying for her to leave after. I don't have time for anything more. Not while I'm busy playing daddy and running my empire.

I pick up my cell phone and dial the number by memory.

"Thank you for calling Allure, the solution to your evening's desires. If you know your party's direct extension—"

A few buttons later, a silky female voice answers. "Hello, Dominic."

"Hello, Gia. How are you today?"

She chuckles in that dark, sultry way of hers. "I'm well, thank you. Reading some fascinating applications at the moment. Yourself?"

"I'm well, but I could use a companion for Friday night's dinner plans."

"Absolutely." Tapping sounds come over the line as she inputs my request. "Tell me what you need."

"Someone intelligent, classy. Someone I can show off to a longtime client and potential investor."

"Always," she says, practically purring. "We'll line up a girl for you in no time at all. I don't have to remind you of our rules . . ."

"Of course not. No sex."

"Unless she wants it, too," she adds with a chuckle. "But knowing your track record, she will."

"You flatterer," I say. Gia, the owner of Allure Agency, certainly knows how to keep her repeat customers satisfied.

"Have a lovely evening, Dom. We'll send you the details tomorrow."

"Good night, Gia."

I set my phone down and lean back in my chair. I already feel better. Excited, even.

After some finishing touches on the day's work, I'm ready to leave. I slip out through the back exit and head directly to the parking garage where my Porsche awaits. I have a small apartment that I keep in the hotel's penthouse suite, but after the babies were born, living out of a hotel seemed much less practical, so I bought a large, four-bedroom apartment where my personal life can stay private and away from the prying eyes of my staff.

Prior to the girls' arrival in my life, I was perfectly happy living a bachelor's lifestyle in a hotel suite—ordering from room service and working at all hours of the day and night. Now, of course, things are different. My priorities have changed drastically.

The commute is never ideal during rush hour, but I want to see my girls. In fact, I *need* to. All of these thoughts about sex, exes, and secret arrangements have me in need of a little emotional cleansing. And there's nothing purer than the glowing smiles of two little girls when their daddy comes home early for the first time all week.

"You ought to spend more time with them. You're missing too much of their childhood," Francine said to me the night before, after I arrived past their bedtime. My nanny is in her late sixties and is never afraid to voice her opinions about my lifestyle. She had her hands on her hips, scolding me like a mother would a child.

"The more time I spend with them, the less you're paid," I reminded her in a stern voice, but she could tell by my smile that it was an empty threat.

I pay her a very generous salary every week, and consistently pay overtime for any extra hours she's needed. What I don't pay her for is unsolicited parental advice. Especially when said advice makes me feel like shit because of how spot-on it is.

"You're lucky my kids are both out of state and my husband has passed on," she said with a wry smile. "I've got nothing better to do than love those little girls."

In the elevator, my heart constricts with emotion, ever so briefly. Even though I've bantered with Fran over the point of my schedule, I know she's right.

My keys aren't even out of the door before I hear the *tap-tap-tap* of little feet on the hardwood floors of my downtown luxury apartment.

"Daddy!" Lacey races down the hall in her dance slippers and barrels right into my legs. Emilia is close behind, her face red and wet with tears.

"There's my girls," I murmur. Kneeling on the floor with two angels in my arms, I smell their hair, feel their tiny hands grasp at my clothes. "What's wrong, baby girl?" I say to Emilia.

"Missed you," she whimpers, clinging to my neck.

"Missed more!" Lacey says.

"It's not a competition, girls," Fran calls from down the hall, hobbling toward me with her coat and purse in hand.

"Thank you," I say. She accepts my gratitude with a wink.

"Glad you're home early for a change," she says in that maternal voice of hers—an influence I've been sorely without for so many years now. "Dinner is on the table."

"Thank you," I say again. I squeeze my daughters tighter against my chest, my nose buried in

Lacey's curls and my fingers tangled in Emilia's. They're my whole life. My everything.

"You should smile more," Fran says as she makes her way to the door, her purse slung over her shoulder and coat already buttoned. "It's very attractive on a young man."

She's right. This is the first time I've smiled since . . . since Presley amused me this morning. It feels like a lifetime ago.

"Say good-bye to Franny," I whisper to the girls. They call out their good-byes, never letting go of me.

Fran chuckles as the door closes softly behind her.

"What's for dinner?" I ask the girls.

"Noodles!" Lacey cries, extracting herself from my arms and running back toward the dining room, but Emilia refuses to let go.

That's all right, little one. I'll carry you.

I sure as hell never thought I'd be a father at twenty-six. I never thought I'd be a single father at all. But I am, and I vow to be a good one. The best

I can possibly be.

Better than mine ever was, at least.

Inside the dining room, I help my twin toddlers into their chairs and survey the table. There's a dish of buttered noodles and peas for my daughters to share, and a plate of baked fish and vegetables for me.

It's another reason why I don't let Francine's meddling bother me. She really does take good care of us and I'm not sure what we'd do without her.

CHAPTER FOUR

Presley

As I enter the cozy, fragrant coffee shop, Michael waves me over to his seat in the corner. *Yes, he even snagged us the super comfy armchairs.* Just seeing him lifts a little of the workday's stress off my shoulders.

He stands up to hug me and points to one of the two steaming mugs on the table. "I ordered you a dirty chai."

"I love you." I sigh.

He shouldn't be using his limited funds to buy me things—heck, I'm paying his tuition, it might be my money in the first place—but after this kind of day, it's nice to have someone remember my favorite drink. We sit down, and I take a grateful sip.

"So, how's school?" I ask. Unable to resist teasing him, I add, "Meet any nice boys yet?"

He groans, though he's still smiling. "I've been too busy getting my ass kicked by this music theory class. Why, have you?" He wiggles his perfectly groomed eyebrows at me.

Okay, I walked into that one. "Not unless you count my new boss," I mutter.

My devastatingly handsome new boss whose ridiculous sex appeal distracted me all damn day. It's so unfair . . . I've never met a guy who lights up my body with electricity from one look, and he's totally off-limits.

"Right, your internship started today. Tell me about that."

"I've only been there one day, so really not much to tell." I sip slowly to cover my nerves.

"You know what I mean. How do you feel about the place?"

"I feel like a blithering idiot." I heave a deep sigh. "It's a once-in-a-lifetime opportunity, and I can't stop worrying I'm going to screw something up and blow it."

"I'm sure you made a great first impression. You always do."

"I don't know . . ."

I stare into my chai as I stir it, imagining my career being sucked into its swirling depths. I must sound as unconvinced as I feel, because Michael pokes my upper arm.

"Hey, pay attention. I'm not just saying that because you're my big sister. You really are the total package."

I force a smile. "Thanks, baby bro."

He frowns—I must sound thoroughly unconvinced—but he lets it go.

"So you said there was a reason you wanted to meet up today?" I ask.

Michael looks supremely uncomfortable. "Yeah . . . well, mostly I just wanted to hang out, but . . . I got a bill from the school a couple days ago, and there's a bunch of extra charges they didn't tell us about before."

Oh, for crying out loud.

"Like what?" I set down my cup. I sense my

composure's about to be tested and don't want to spill my drink everywhere.

"Um, like transportation, athletics, a studio fee for my conditioning class, campus fee, orientation fee . . . I forget what else. It listed like a half dozen things."

What the hell is a campus fee? Is that the price you pay to be able to attend class on school grounds? What does tuition even pay for if all this stuff isn't covered?

I rub my forehead to ward off the impending stress headache. I'm afraid to ask, but I have to. "How much?"

He hesitates, averting his gaze. "Nineteen hundred dollars."

Forget spilling my chai; I might have thrown it across the room if it were still in my hand. Almost two freaking grand—when I can barely afford an extra cup of coffee a week.

I close my eyes and pull in a deep breath. "Okay."

I'll figure this out. I have no freaking idea how, because I already had nothing to live off of for the next three months except my meager savings. But I'll come up with something.

You never know . . . maybe Dominic will decide you've failed the trial period and fire you after only two weeks.

"Y-you don't have to pay the full amount. Some of it is optional." Michael rushes to explain, his hands raised in placation. "Like for my choreography class, we're putting on a performance at the end of the semester, so they're charging us for costumes and theater time and stuff. But I can always just drop that class and—"

"No. Don't worry, I'll get the money." *Somehow . . .*

"Okay, if you're sure . . . thanks a million. I'll pay you back someday."

I catch the subtle sparkle in Michael's eyes. He's clearly excited about that performance, which only hardens my resolve.

I can do this. I have to.

"You don't owe me anything," I say, squeezing his arm. "We're family. If we don't look out for each other, who will?" Not our father, that's for damn sure.

Michael's pocket beeps and he checks his phone. "Whoops. I hate to ditch you, but the last bus back to my dorm will be here in five minutes. Love you, sis!"

"Love you, too," I say, standing again for a good-bye hug.

Now what? I was just starting to feel better about work, but after hearing about Michael's surprise expenses, I'm wound tighter than ever. I'm hungry, and since I'm not done with my drink yet and I'm in desperate need of something to eat, I head to the counter and order their last slice of banana bread.

"We're mortal enemies now," someone says from behind me.

I glance back, bewildered.

The guy in line behind me grins. "I wanted the last slice."

"Oh, I'm sorry. Do you want—"

"Don't worry about it, I was just kidding. Heh . . . I guess it was a bad joke." He points to my table, which still has all my stuff on it. "By the way, is that sticker on your laptop from *Delinquent Story?* I love that webcomic."

"Wow, really?" I say, more than a little surprised. "You're the first person I've met who's even heard of it."

His brown eyes crinkle in the corners when he smiles at me, his messy brown hair flopping over one eye when he nods. "What did you think of the part where—actually, maybe I should invite you to sit down before I start asking questions." He gestures to a two-person table that's been staked out with a messenger bag on one chair.

He has a nice smile. What the heck, I could use a friend right about now. "Sure, thanks."

He helps me move my stuff to his table. In between bites and sips, I rave about my favorite webcomic for almost twenty minutes while he nods, murmurs in agreement, and eggs me on with the occasional question.

"Plus, the art style is so nuanced. Like, Sheri's expressions are exaggerated while Lila's are subtle and ambiguous to show the—" I cut myself off, suddenly realizing I'm being rude. "S-sorry, I've just been going on and on. I haven't even asked your name."

He chuckles. "No worries, I was really interested in what you were saying. I'm Austin."

"I'm Presley. So, what do you do?" I ask.

"I'm a programmer. You?"

"I actually just started a new job at Aspen today." I polish off the last bite of my banana bread and wipe my mouth with a napkin.

Austin's eyebrows wing up. "Wow, the massive hotel chain? I've heard they're really competitive."

"No kidding. To tell you the truth, I don't quite feel like I belong there."

I'm not sure why I'm saying all this. I practically just met this guy, and I'm pouring out my insecurities. But he's such a good listener, it feels like I can tell him what's on my mind.

"It's probably just first-day jitters," he says. "It'll wear off when you get used to the people and how they do things. You seem smart, and you wouldn't have gotten the job in the first place if they didn't think you were good enough."

"That's true." I chuckle and shake my head. "Sorry to make you play therapist."

"You didn't make me do anything. I said that because I wanted to." He smiles back, a little shy, but genuine. "Listen, I gotta run, but can I have your number? And maybe we can meet up for coffee again sometime? I mean, you do kinda owe me a slice of banana bread . . ."

I consider, but it doesn't take much thought. He's easy to talk to, and his candid manner is both comfortable and refreshing. He's also cute—not like Dominic's overpowering, slightly intimidating magnetism, but in a sweet, safe, boy-next-door kind of way. Austin is exactly what I need to get these forbidden feelings off my mind.

Pulling out my phone, I smile. "Sure, I'd like that."

After I leave the coffee shop, all I can think about the entire way home is the bill Michael hit me with. I tried to keep my cool in front of him, but the truth is, I'm freaking out about how I'm going to do all this.

Bianca's not home when I reach the apartment, and I remember the yoga class she takes on Monday nights. So I grab a handful of nuts that I hope will tide me over, and open my laptop to continue working on the notes I started putting together for my business proposal.

There's nothing else I can do besides get down to work. Besides, there's no sense in worrying about my money problems when I have a CEO to impress.

• • •

I make it through Aspen's doors at eight o'clock sharp, and I've barely sat down at my desk when Jordan pokes his head into my cubicle.

"Hey . . . Parsley, right?"

"Presley." I sigh.

"Oh shit, I'm so sorry." He lets out a nervous laugh. "Oliver says he wants us to develop a budget proposal for the new Acapulco resort. Can you meet now? Or I can come back later . . ."

Why assign us together? Never mind, it doesn't matter. Dominic gave me my own duties, but if Aspen's vice president wants me to do something, that's what I'm going to do. Maybe this is intended to test how well we juggle multiple tasks or handle teamwork or something. Regardless, I'm sure it's some kind of test, and I'll be damn sure that I ace it.

I follow Jordan to his cubicle, where he pulls up a long email from Oliver and leaves me to read it while he finds a second chair.

As we work, my initial bad impression of Jordan fades. Sure, he lacks rigor—his habit of not double-checking the company style guide drives me nuts—but his observations are insightful and his suggestions creative.

Around eleven, my stomach growls so loudly, I swear it echoes off the walls. Blushing, I say, "Sorry, I missed breakfast."

Jordan laughs, not unkindly. "You wanna take an early lunch?"

"I guess we're at a good spot for a break."

Still chatting about our joint project, we head to the employee cafeteria, load up our trays, and find seats. In between thoughts, I scarf down my chicken salad sandwich and barbecue chips, feeling very grateful that this internship includes a free lunch.

The way Jordan tips his chair back while he eats makes me nervous; I get the feeling that if we weren't at work, he'd prop his feet on the table. I'm not nearly as comfortable here.

Out of nowhere, he says, "So, Dominic, huh? What's it like working directly with the big bad CEO himself?"

I finish chewing and consider his question. "His approach to business seems pretty bold. He also has really high standards. Which I respect, because he holds himself to those standards, too. I saw his calendar once, and he's scheduled within an inch of his life. But it's hard work to keep up with how demanding he is, and sometimes he can be a little too blunt."

Don't forget hotter than sin, my libido nags.

"Man, that sounds intense." Jordan sucks his teeth in sympathy. "I wonder why we got assigned the way we did. Like you and Dominic—you think maybe he picked you to mentor because you're hot?"

Excuse me? Hell no, I did not just hear that.

"What the hell kind of question is that?" I just

barely stop myself from shouting at him, and the words come out as a strangled hiss. I can't believe this guy was starting to grow on me.

Jordan's eyes go huge. "Oh shit, I didn't mean it like that! I'm sure you got this internship fair and square. You definitely know your stuff. Dominic's the one I wonder about. Y'know, with his . . . quirk."

I throw my hands up in exasperation. "What are you talking about?"

"Huh? You didn't know? Haven't heard the rumors yet?"

"What rumors?" I ask, lowering my voice and leaning in close.

Jordan grins crookedly at the knowledge he knows something I don't. "That he pays for sex," he whispers back.

My mouth drops open. "S-seriously?"

"I know, right? He doesn't seem like the type. But I heard it straight from Oliver, so I don't think it's just an empty rumor." Jordan tosses back a few fries and chews noisily.

"You heard that straight from Oliver?" It seems highly unlikely for the vice president to be gossiping about his own boss. Or unprofessional at the very least.

Jordan just shrugs. "Well, *overheard*, I guess you could say. He was taking a personal phone call when I happened to walk into his office for our meeting."

I stare down at my food like it can provide me with answers. But holy hell, am I supposed to act normal around *my very hot boss* with this indecent knowledge rattling around in my head? I'm not supposed to know this much about his private business.

I grab the rest of my lunch, mumbling, "I just remembered some emails I have to send. I'm going to finish eating at my desk." My cheeks burn as I stalk off.

CHAPTER FIVE

Dominic

I can't focus. My fingers drum an unsteady beat on my desk as I listen to Oliver rattle off our executive task list for this quarter. One task requires me to go to a dinner with this potential investor of ours tonight.

If I'm being frank, I couldn't care less about impressing this man today. The only thing that's leaving any impression on me is my zipper on my permanent hard-on. All week, I've been at the end of my goddamn rope. Seeing Presley's tight little body, smelling her vanilla shampoo, hearing her warm-honey voice, watching her knock every assignment out of the ballpark. . .

It's been insanely distracting, and I'm not proud of myself for it. All I need right now is a good hard fuck to flush out all of these unneeded impulses.

". . . and after we build the spaceship and fly it around the world at least twice, we can go get our assholes waxed."

"What?" I finally break out of my reverie, staring blankly at my best friend, but Oliver only raises his eyebrows. "Oh, sorry. Shit."

"Hey, Dom. Didn't know you were still here." Oliver tosses his folder onto my desk. "Look, man, if you don't want to talk work, let's not talk work. That's the last thing I want to talk about anyway."

"All right. What do you want to talk about?"

"How about we talk about how uptight you've been ever since you took on your hot little intern?"

Shit. "My stress level has nothing to do with Presley."

"Right, just like my dad's late nights had nothing to do with his smoking-hot consultant. Come on, Dom. You like her, just admit it." He smiles, his eyebrows waggling.

"I *like* her? What are we, twelve?"

"You know what I mean." He sighs and props

his feet on the edge of my desk.

I hate it when he does this. I frown at the prospect of scrubbing those scuff marks away again.

"I really don't," I grumble, using his folder to swat his feet off my desk. "Don't feel obliged to elaborate."

"Don't feel obliged to elaborate." He mimics me like the little prick he can be. "Oh, I'll elaborate all right. You wanna fuck her. You want to turn her over on this very desk, spread her legs, and ram it home. You want to fill her with your—"

"Okay, Jesus, do you have to be so . . ." I can't find any word that won't make me sound like my father. *Crass? Inappropriate? Childish?* But, fuck, I am a father now, strange as that still seems to me.

Oliver laughs, then lets out a sigh as he suddenly sobers. "You can't fuck her, though."

"I know that. I'm not going to." This isn't a college frat party.

The look on his face tells me he's not buying any of my bullshit.

"I'm not," I say. "I'm just fucking horny. But

I've got it covered. I've got a date lined up."

"A date?" Oliver's eyes widen with hope.

"No, not a date." *Damn*. I shouldn't have used that word. Oliver wants me to seriously commit myself to someone. It was cruel of me to dangle that bone in front of him. "I have an arrangement."

"Oh, one of those arrangements. Like, you're-fucking-a-hooker arrangement."

"They aren't hookers, they're *escorts*. 'Hooker' has a very negative connotation. And sex isn't part of the arrangement, it's—"

"It's just an added benefit," Oliver says, finishing my sentence for me.

Right, he's heard all of this before. No need to try to enlighten a friend who isn't capable of understanding my survival mechanisms. But it's my life, not his, and I get to live it however I see fit. I'd like to see him try to keep two toddlers alive, and run a corporation. Paying for sex is the least of my worries.

"I don't get it." Shaking his head, Oliver studies me like he's reading my mind. "But I accept you."

Finally. I chuckle. My vice president may be the only person left in my life that I trust, despite our differences. I barely trust myself like this. But tonight, I'll get that unpredictable side of me under control.

Tonight, I'll fuck any thoughts of Presley right out of my system.

And I can't fucking wait.

• • •

In the car on the way home from the gym, I'm still tense. My fingers squeeze the wheel, my knuckles whitening. Even my chest feels tight.

Seriously?

I doubled my usual reps and tripled my usual mileage. Still, I couldn't shake this feeling. I have too much energy. Too much gas in the tank, as my mother would say. A smile quirks my lips at the memory of Mom watching Teddy and me run laps around the kitchen table, shaking her head in dismay. When we were young, I was always chasing my brother, my hero—

Teddy.

No time for that train of thought. I speed down the road, eyeing the clock. If I make it home in the next five minutes, I may catch the girls before they're tucked in bed for the night.

I'm only minutes too late, it turns out. When I open the door to my penthouse apartment, I don't hear the familiar sound of tiny feet pitter-pattering down the hall. Instead, I hear the soft thud of Fran's steady footfalls on the wood floor.

"Just put them to bed," she whispers. "They were tuckered out from the park."

"Thank you for taking them. I wish I could have gone instead."

Fran says nothing to that, only hums thoughtfully to herself. I can tell she's biting her tongue, wanting to say something about my work schedule conflicting with my child rearing.

I clench my jaw, accepting that she has a right to judge. I could be better. That much is true. And I'll always try to be a better version of myself. I may not be perfect now—not at work, or at home—but I won't let that keep me from striving for it.

I may not be able to be in two places at the same time, but I can absolutely be two different men—the tough and decisive CEO during the day, and the good father at night. I have to be. There's really no other choice.

After Fran has waddled into the living room to sit with her knitting, I take off my shoes and head into my daughters' room to find them curled up together in Lacey's bed. My heart squeezes as I watch them. It's sweet how they can't bear to be apart, even when sleeping.

I step closer and gaze down at their little faces. They're already sound asleep, little eyelashes fluttering with dreams. *Good ones, I hope.* I lean down and press a kiss onto each of their foreheads.

God, I wish I could just crawl into bed with them and curl up under these cashmere blankets. Let myself rest for even a moment and indulge in the simplicity of childhood bliss.

But I can't. I have to get dressed. I have to put on my game face and impress this client.

I slowly stand and walk toward the door. After peering at them once more through the crack, I pull the door closed behind me.

Daddy's got work to do.

CHAPTER SIX

Presley

I spoil myself, ordering a fourteen-dollar glass of champagne. When it's placed before me in a glass flute, I take a slow sip, letting the bubbles dance over my tongue as I silently congratulate myself on a great first week of work. In a few years, I'll be able to order bottles of this stuff and not bat an eyelash at the cost, and I'll be able to make sure Michael has what he needs. I just have to keep working hard.

Since Bianca has a date tonight, and I didn't feel like going home alone to an apartment that's not even mine, I've stationed myself at a bar around the corner from the hotel. I slowly sip my drink, savoring it since I probably won't be able to order myself something so extravagant for the foreseeable future.

A deep voice rumbles a curse, and something about the sound of the man's voice makes me turn. Seated to my left, about six bar stools down, is Dominic Aspen.

Heat floods my cheeks at the sight of him. Even if this is one of the closest bars to the hotel where we both work, I never expected to see him here.

Correction: I work there. He owns it. It's crazy to think that this man employs close to forty-thousand people around the globe.

He's clearly upset about something, and I watch in fascination as he stabs at the screen of his phone, typing out a hurried message.

Dominic pushes one hand through his hair and then finishes his whiskey neat in a single gulp. He looks up and our eyes meet, and my cheeks flush with heat when I realize I've been watching him.

"Presley?" His deep voice is raspy and sends goose bumps skittering down my spine.

I take a healthy gulp of my champagne and then carry my glass down to join him. "Hello, Mr. Aspen."

"Call me Dominic."

I nod. "Are you enjoying happy hour?" I ask, and then instantly curse myself for how childish that sounded. I'm sure he already sees me as some know-nothing coed, and that little remark probably just reinforced that idea. *Idiot*.

"What? No." He shakes his head. "I have a business dinner starting in thirty minutes around the corner, and I was supposed to meet my date here."

"Oh." My hands fall into my lap. Of course he has a date, a beautiful man like him. After all, it's Friday night. I'm the only weirdo with no plans. I tip my head, looking down at my scuffed shoes. "Have fun, then. I won't keep you."

I finish the last of my champagne and rise to my feet, fishing around inside my purse until I locate my wallet.

Dominic frowns at me. "Sit down, Presley."

Before I can even process his request, my body is obeying, and I lower myself back onto the bar stool.

Dominic catches the bartender's attention to order me a second glass of bubbly, and requests my check be given to him. "My date canceled tonight," he says at my obvious confusion.

"Oh. I'm sorry to hear that." My heart pumps faster.

"So am I."

He seems a little annoyed by this and looks down into his now-empty glass. I can't help but notice he didn't order himself another drink. Maybe because he needs to be clearheaded at his business dinner.

When my second drink arrives, it tastes even better than the first. Maybe because there's a gorgeous man sitting next to me. Or maybe it's because he's one of the most powerful men in the world; his net worth has many zeroes behind it.

The sight of my polished, hypercompetent boss admitting he was stood up makes my heart squeeze. "I can't imagine what kind of woman would cancel on you," I say, and then immediately wish I could shove the words back inside my mouth.

Dominic's eyes are bright with curiosity as he appraises me. "I've never met her before, actually. It was a setup."

Jordan's words about Dominic Aspen "paying for it" ring in my head.

"So the rumors about you are true?" Apparently, my tongue has been loosened by the alcohol, because I really have no excuse for my boldness right now.

Dominic's dark eyebrows raise. "Rumors?"

I clear my throat, my posture straightening. "That you *acquire* your dates."

His lips twitch, and he smiles. "I have an agency that supplies me with dates. Don't look so scandalized, it's the era of dating apps and swiping left, after all"

I nod. "I see. Well, I'm sorry that you were stood up."

He nods once, watching me take another sip of my champagne. "Why are you sorry? Are you offering to fill in and help me?"

"M-me?" I stutter. "I couldn't."

Dominic turns to face me, giving me a pleading look, and something twists inside of me. "I've been trying to court this investor for months now, and

I finally managed to snag a dinner meeting with him."

Which means we wouldn't have to be alone together. There's a third wheel in the mix—probably some old guy, but still, a chaperone. A confusing mix of relief and disappointment rushes over me.

"I'm going to be honest," he says. "I *really* need to show up to this dinner with a beautiful woman on my arm. I've already made the reservation for three, so if I show up alone, it'll look like I've been ditched. Not very impressive on first impressions and all."

"For the sake of appearances," I say slowly, still trying to wrap my head around the idea of *me* acting as someone's trophy date. The idea is pretty absurd.

"Exactly. And if we can impress this guy, Aspen stands to gain a lot. Fifty million dollars, to be precise." He sighs, then presses his lips into a tight line. "I promise I won't let it affect our work relationship if you say no . . . but please, at least consider it."

As if our work relationship isn't already "affected." Dear God, things at the office have gotten

ten thousand times more complicated than I ever imagined.

Part of me is flattered that he said *we* instead of *I*, as if we both have an equal role in impressing this important investor. But I can't help wondering if Dominic would expect something more of me . . . assuming his date was also someone he planned to sleep with.

No, it couldn't be. Right? And even on the off chance he does, I would never sleep with my boss. No matter how smoking hot he looks in that custom-tailored suit.

I drop my gaze, chewing my lip. "I don't know."

"It's one client dinner, Presley. And I'll pay you for your time. There's nothing improper about it."

He's right. It's not like he's not asking me out. It's a work event, one I would have readily agreed to if he'd asked me during business hours.

"Five hundred dollars for your evening. What do you say?"

Five hundred dollars is a lot of money, money that would really help with the bill Michael just gave me.

Briefly, I wonder what the other interns would say if they knew I was out with Dominic. Then again, I suppose it would be no different than if Jordan went to dinner, or say, golfing with Oliver. It's all part of business, right? I could think of it like working overtime. Plus, the benefit of spending more time with the CEO himself, and the chance to see how business deals are made, would be a huge advantage to my long-term goals with Aspen.

I have to say yes. And it has nothing to do with how gorgeously attractive the man seated next to me is. Or how his deep voice washes over me, making my stomach twist with nerves.

"Well, I have to leave in three minutes to make the reservation, so I'm afraid I need a quick decision."

I take a deep breath, trying to compose myself. This could be a huge opportunity. I'll have a front-row seat to the details that could affect the whole business. It's a chance to observe and learn from two of the biggest players around. If I manage not to put my foot in my mouth, I might even be able to have some small effect on their decisions.

On top of that, I can't help feeling a little sad

for Dominic. He's stuck between a rock and a hard place right now.

With a deep, steadying breath, I rise to my feet. "I still have no idea if I can do this, but I'll try."

"That's a good life philosophy. Brave . . ." He checks his watch and gives me a slight smirk. "And decisive, too. You had an extra minute to spare."

"Thanks. Will you hold it against me if I have to bail halfway through?" My voice almost quavers, but not quite, and I count it as a small victory.

He looks amused as he fishes out his wallet and hands a couple of large bills to the bartender. "Not if you come up with a decent excuse. In business school, this girl stood me up twice, and both times she claimed her roommate died."

A giggle escapes me. I'm still so nervous, I feel a little breathless, but if he's trying to set me at ease, it's helping a little. Still, I can't help but wonder if the girl he's talking about was a real date or a hired escort. I can't ask that, though, can I?

Just because we're spending time together outside of work doesn't mean I'm comfortable with him. Far from it. This man exudes confidence and power and raw sex appeal. And I'm trying my hardest not to notice that last one.

Dominic leads the way to the front of the bar and then holds open the heavy glass door for me. I step past him, and then we face each other on the sidewalk. He just looks at me for a moment, and I'm not sure what to say.

"Am I dressed okay?" I finally settle on, unable to take the intensity of his scrutiny any longer. I'm still dressed for work—black suit pants, white button-down shirt, a red cardigan over that.

His mouth twitches with the hint of a smile. "You look very proper." Softening his tone, he adds, "I hope I didn't hijack your evening."

I shake my head. "I didn't have any plans. Other than maybe getting a head start on my new project."

Dominic chuckles and nods toward the sidewalk. "Will you be okay to walk in those heels? The restaurant is four blocks in that direction. If not, I'm happy to get a car, whatever you prefer."

Maybe that's why he was looking at me. To determine if I could make it four blocks without breaking my ankle in my high heels.

"I can walk."

"Perfect."

We start off, and since I don't usually walk this way, I'm busy cataloging the little bakeries, cafés, and gift shops that I'll probably never get to enjoy. At least, not until I'm pulling in a bigger paycheck. Putting my brother through school is every bit as difficult as I feared it would be. I just need to stay focused.

As we walk, I'm desperate to break the silence, and search for some small-talk topic that will keep us occupied.

"So, you're not dating anyone?" I settle on.

"God, no."

He answers so fast, I actually giggle. "Jeez. I didn't ask if you had the plague."

Dominic smiles warmly at me. "I'm too busy to date."

I return his smile. "I know the feeling. At this stage in my life, the only thing I want to focus on is my career."

He nods. "That's very admirable."

We reach the restaurant with its glass-and-chrome doors, and Dominic stops with his hand extended.

"Appearances, remember?" he murmurs, his voice deep and silky. "When I said I need a woman on my arm, I meant it literally."

I swallow, then place my hand in his. His palm is warm and solid and engulfs mine completely. It's a little disorienting.

As we enter together, I can't resist sneaking a peek at him. I've never set foot in such an opulent restaurant. The red carpeting is thick beneath my heels, and crystal chandeliers hang from the ceiling. Each table is draped with a creamy linen tablecloth and bears a vase of fiery orchids.

Dominic greets the hostess and gives her his name. She leads us to an intimate curved booth where an older man sits drinking a glass of red wine. He looks to be in his fifties, with a slight paunch and a neat fringe of salt-and-pepper hair around his ears.

He stands up to shake hands with Dominic.

"Great to see you again. As you can tell, I got here a few minutes early and decided to get a head start on the evening." He chuckles at his own joke.

Giving him my best customer-service smile, I offer my hand and he shakes it. "Hello, I'm Presley."

"A pleasure to meet you, miss. I'm Roger." Then he looks at Dominic. "Boy, you just keep getting them younger, don't you?"

It takes effort not to let my face fall. *Jeez . . .*

Dominic's expression stays pleasant, but the look he gives Roger is razor sharp. "Presley is only four years younger than me, actually. She also happens to be brilliant. She went to Brown University on full scholarship, she's interned at several of the Northwest's top companies in finance and leadership, and in high school, she won the national coding competition four years in a row."

Roger and I both blink at him, stunned. Butterflies fill my stomach. Dominic has every reason to flatter this guy, but I secretly like the way he leaped in to defend me.

And how did he remember all that stuff? Dominic has my résumé, it makes sense that he'd know everything about my career accomplishments, but I'm surprised he can rattle off so much from memory. The warmth in my chest grows at the thought.

Roger clears his throat. "That, ah . . . yes, that's quite the list. Should we have a seat and order some dinner?"

Dominic's lips twitch with the hint of a smile. "Perfect," he replies in a sunny tone. "I'm looking forward to getting down to details, but first we need some refills on drinks." He nods to Roger's wineglass, which is half-empty.

We sit, with Dominic between Roger and me. I try not to look visibly shocked at the prices as I study the menu.

Dominic leans close. "What would you like to drink?"

It's unnerving having him so close, but not entirely unwelcome. His crisp, masculine scent—leather, and cedar, and something I can't name washes over me, and the heat from his thigh is so close.

"Um . . ." It's hard to think with him almost

touching me . . . not to mention that deep, smooth voice practically murmuring in my ear. "Is there a white wine here you recommend?" Hopefully that sounds sophisticated enough to mask the fact that I usually just grab whatever has the smallest price tag.

"They have a pinot gris that's quite good. I'll order us both a glass." In a softer tone, he adds, "You're doing fine, by the way." Then he pats my knee reassuringly under the table.

I almost gasp when his touch sends an electric jolt straight up my thigh and beyond.

He's just being nice, I sternly tell myself. *Absolutely platonic*. But my body doesn't care. It reacts the same way it would if any attractive, eligible man were touching it.

Pressing my knees together, I force my attention back to the menu.

CHAPTER SEVEN

Dominic

Presley leans in as she speaks, her eyes sparkling along with the candlelight and crystal of the dimly lit restaurant. She's telling Roger all about the ballet programs in the city.

For the very first time, I'm the speechless one. Usually, my escort keeps her words to a minimum, sprinkling in the occasional nod and laugh. But Presley has me beat for Roger's attention.

"Really, I think Julie would love it. Especially if she's inclined toward dance," she says, placing an encouraging hand on the table between them.

"She is definitely chock-full of energy, that kid." Roger's granddaughter is five, and his wife keeps her after school on weekdays. From what he's told us, she's a little terror. Rampaging around the house, breaking things both accidentally and on purpose. "Meanwhile, I find myself running lower and lower on energy every day."

He raises his glass to us. "Not that you younger people can relate. You don't have to worry about kids for years," he says with a wistful sigh.

I snort, to which both Presley and Roger turn.

"Thank God," I say, covering smoothly, and I tip my glass toward his. We clink our drinks together, and I can see Presley eyeing me inquisitively over her wine.

"To preserving energy," I say.

"To ballet," Presley responds, and Roger laughs heartily. If I haven't won him over, my date certainly has. And how could she not? She's gorgeous, smart, funny . . .

My intern turned escort.

I mentally chastise myself. I'm not dating Presley. *Don't get too comfy with this, Dom.*

It's easy to talk to her, easy to work with her. She's young and bright and beautiful, but that doesn't mean I get to picture how her pouty mouth would look taking my cock, or get myself all jacked up on her pheromones—no matter how good she smells, or how warm she is sitting beside me.

I've seen interest flickering in her gaze when our eyes meet, but still, Oliver is right. I can't fuck her. Which really puts a damper on tonight.

I lean in and try to compose myself. "Roger, tell me. What's your opinion on a financial partnership with us?" Okay, so this was a little more straightforward of an approach than Ollie would have suggested, but I'm rolling with it.

"You'll have to tell me more." He leans back against the tufted booth. "What kind of partnership are you thinking?"

"You've been a longtime client of Aspen. And you're a consistent customer at my hotel, in particular, and a pleasure to do business with. Your last company-wide reservation put us right in the margins that we needed to be in. It's been incredibly profitable for us, and we want to return the favor."

"I'm listening."

"If Roger Harwood, LLC invests in a small share of Aspen Hotels, we can assure you an even better deal than what you're getting."

"Your father told me I was already getting the best deal there was." Roger swirls the ruby-colored wine in his glass.

"That may have been true at the time. But I'm not quite as shortsighted as my father," I say with a smile. "Dad had goals but didn't execute them outside of his comfort zone."

"What kind of goals are you talking about?"

"International goals," I say, and he sits up a little straighter. "I know you have a lot of business out of the country, and I can assure you that once our international locations are funded, all Harwood employees can enjoy the benefits of being friends of Aspen Hotels."

As I lay out the details of the deal, I can feel Presley's gaze on me. For the first time during the dinner, she's completely still, her eyes locked on my face, watching my lips.

Fuck, that's distracting. What is she thinking about?

"Presley, what do you think?" Roger asks, turning to her.

She returns his gaze and smiles warmly. "I think it's a fucking good deal," she says, then glances at me as if to ask, *Too much?*

I can't help the smile spreading across my lips, and I chuckle.

Roger outright erupts into laughter. "A fucking good deal!"

"Let me try that again." Presley grins, her eyes bright. She places her hands on the table in front of her, and proceeds to blow us away with her knowledge of Aspen Hotels and how Roger could benefit from this deal.

Grinning, Roger leans forward. "Where did you find her?" he asks me.

Swallowing, I meet Presley's eyes, and have to mentally compose myself, because fuck. I've never been this turned on in my life and she's nowhere near my dick. Not to mention she's still fully clothed.

Roger reaches over the table and we shake hands warmly, exchanging promises of setting up a formal meeting soon to double-check logistics and nail down the details. I'm confident that we can satisfy this man's goals while exceeding our own financial plans.

Dinner is long done and our glasses are empty. It's time to wrap things up. As we get up to leave, Roger extends a hand to Presley, who accepts with a firm shake.

"Thank you, Presley, for sharing your evening with me," he says with genuine kindness in his voice.

Presley smiles warmly. "Anytime, Roger. I'll be around."

Her statement is curious. Is she trying to make him think we're dating? I didn't exactly dissuade him from the idea. What other logical conclusion could he have drawn?

• • •

After dinner, I call a car and we slip inside. The silence in the limo is deafening. How did we go from such friendly conversation to complete silence?

Having an idea why, I clear my throat softly. "You don't have to be uncomfortable."

She nearly jumps at the sound of my voice.

Nice work, Dom.

"Don't I?" Presley asks, laughing softly.

"I understand if you are."

"No, I . . . I'm uncomfortable with how easy it was."

"How do you mean?"

"Sitting there, talking business. Flattering the client. Being your date."

There's that word again. Why don't I want to correct her when she uses it?

"You were good at it," I say in a low voice. Arousal stirs in my veins, and I take a breath to remind myself why this is a terrible idea.

"Thank you," she says with a soft smile. Even in the dark of the limo, I can see her eyes sparkle. "It was my first time. Doing something like this, I mean."

She's a good girl, just as I suspected. She's probably never broken one rule, done anything outside of her straight-A, Miss Responsible routine in her entire life. So, why does that thought make me want to bend her over my desk and spank her ass?

"Really? I couldn't tell," I say, trying to keep my tone cool.

"No, I just wasn't sure how it would go. Pretending with you, I mean," she says, wringing her hands. "I'm sorry, I shouldn't be so chatty about this with you. Duh."

She's so fucking cute.

"It's no trouble. I'm interested."

"Well, thanks. I'm glad you were my first." She blushes immediately. "I don't mean that, like, sexually. I've never had a first— I mean— Shit." She buries her face in her clutch with a groan. Her voice is muffled when she says, "Can you pretend I didn't just say that?"

"Sure."

I say one thing, but as usual, my body does another. My cock sure can't forget that little piece of treasured knowledge.

Presley hasn't had sex? Unless I misunderstood

her, I think she just implied she's a virgin. She's never fucked anyone? Never been fucked? With each racing question, my dick pulses.

Well, shit.

This dinner was incredibly successful on the business front. Not exactly a personal victory for the front of my pants, however. I'm still as horny as fuck, if not more than before. *Goddammit.*

We pull up to her apartment complex. I climb out of the car, walk around, and open her door. She quietly steps out. The distance between us is maddening, but I maintain it all the same.

"Have a good night," she says softly, almost breathless.

Am I making you nervous, Presley?

"You're not done with me yet." I offer her my arm.

"Oh, I'm not—"

"Don't worry. I just want to walk you to your door."

"Oh. All right." She bites her lip, stifling a soft laugh, as she loops her arm through mine.

I can't remember the last time I walked a woman to her door. It's certainly not something I do when I'm out with an escort. It should bother me that this feels much more like a date than It should. Presley's my employee, for Christ's sake. But I guess I'm still riding a high of how well she did winning over Roger.

We walk in silence up to her apartment door. It reminds me of where I lived in college, an old brick and mortar with a buzzer next to the door. Nostalgia fills me with a thousand memories of the younger me. Bold. Reckless. Carefree.

It seems like a lifetime ago.

I hold her hand up the steps until we reach the top, enjoying how soft her skin is as it rests lightly against my palm. At the door, she turns back to me. I'm on the stair below, our eyes at the same level. For a moment, we just take in the sight of each other. She really is beautiful with her high cheek-bones, wide eyes, and full mouth.

"Thank you, Dominic. I had a nice time." It's almost a whisper. She isn't quite looking in my eyes anymore, but rather her gaze rests on my lips.

Interesting.

"No. Thank you," I say softly.

Her hand is still in mine, and I lift it to the lips she's been staring at to press a chaste kiss to the back of her hand. I swear I can feel her take in a breath. With my lips still touching her, I meet her eyes.

A blush spreads across her cheeks. "See you at work," I murmur.

Moments later, I climb into the limo. I settle into my seat, watching as Presley unlocks her apartment door and steps inside.

"Home, sir?" my driver asks.

"Yes, home."

• • •

"Poke him."

"I did."

"Again."

A tiny finger nudges my Adam's apple. My eyes open, still hazy with sleep.

God, how long was I out?

I squint against the morning light streaming through my bedroom window. Lacey's honey-colored curls float into view. She and Emilia are on their tippy-toes, reaching for me with their chubby little arms.

"You better not poke the bear," I grumble. "In the morning, the bear is hungry!"

I launch out of bed with a growl, sending my toddlers scrambling away with yelps of joy. With the blanket wrapped around my shoulders, I stomp down the hall.

Lacey yells, "Run!" and Emilia cries out, "Hide!"

I chuckle as I follow them. God, they're fucking cute. Even if I'm not ready to be awake yet.

They both scramble into the kitchen, hiding in plain sight under the dining table. I make an effort not to look, sniffing the air and circling around them with big, loud steps.

"Where are my little cubs? They must be so hungry . . ."

"We're hungry! We're cubs!"

They both crawl out from under the table, grasping at my legs. I let them pull me to the floor where I sit cross-legged and wrap them in my arms. Their familiar smell . . . their familiar weight against my chest . . . this is all I need, right here in my arms.

"You know what? You smell like . . . pancakes!" I snarl into Emilia's neck, who screams with excitement.

Lacey's eyes grow wide. "Pancakes!"

Pancakes, it is.

The rest of my morning will consist of making pancakes the way my mother taught me—one at a time, with a little butter in the pan. After breakfast, I'll spend a good twenty minutes wiping maple syrup off their chins and fingers. Then when I take them to the park, Emilia will inevitably find some way to hurt herself. But that won't be a problem, because I'll carry her home.

After that, we'll eat lunch. Mac and cheese, their favorite. Then it'll be board games and a nap before dinner, and finally story time. Something about a princess, I'm sure.

It's another full day of just another kind of work. But I wouldn't trade it for all the free time in the world.

CHAPTER EIGHT

Presley

Poking her brush at the paper, Bianca mutters, "This looks like ass."

I glance at her perfectly decent watercolor landscape. "Hey, you're doing better than me. My trees clearly have some kind of disease."

She's always been the more artistic one. It was her idea to spend our lazy Saturday afternoon sipping cheap wine at a nearby painting studio that offers classes. Not that I objected—after the week I've had, the instructor's hypnotically calm voice is more than welcome, and the act of painting is also soothing, despite how much I suck at it. Plus, Bianca's mother bought her a gift card here last Christmas, and so this little excursion doesn't hurt my pocketbook.

We mix and dab in comfortable silence for a while before Bianca asks, "So how'd your first week at the new job go?"

I hesitate, the tip of my brush hovering over a lumpy cloud. "Actually . . . something weird happened last night."

"Why were you working so late? I thought you were going out for a drink."

"I wasn't working. Well, I sort of was, just not at work."

"You can start making sense whenever, y'know." Her brush drips paint on the carpet, but no one seems to notice.

I take a deep breath. "I saw Dominic at the bar, and he said . . . he needed somebody to go to a business dinner with him. The person he invited ditched him." I probably don't need to mention the detail about how he hires women for sex. "He offered me five-hundred dollars, so I went."

Now it's Bianca's turn to pause. She stares at her painting, her brow furrowing deeper and deeper, then she looks at me. "Your boss paid you to be his date." Her tone is dead flat.

I pause to listen to the instructor's next instructions before replying. "O-okay, I get how that sounds bad, but it wasn't really a *date*, per se, he just—"

"Asked you to dinner?" she says icily.

"It's not like we were alone together. There was an investor—the point of everything was to try to impress him. Strictly business. I would have done it for free, the money was just because it was such short notice."

She purses her lips, then makes a low, grudging noise. "Well . . . as long as this isn't some gross sexual harassment thing, I guess I don't have to kill him."

"I'm pretty sure it's not." No matter how much I sometimes wish it were, except there's nothing gross about Dominic Aspen. "Anyway, I think it went well. The investor seemed happy. I hope it was enough to convince him that Aspen is a worthwhile bet."

"Great, but I'm still skeptical about whether this was the best idea," Bianca says.

"I know it's . . . unorthodox. But I figured, hey, I

can make a little extra money for Michael's school stuff, learn more about business, and get extra access to the CEO. I'm competing with three other highly qualified interns, so why not take advantage of a chance to push ahead?"

"Those are all good points." Bianca smirks. "And I'm sure that you having the hots for Dominic has nothing to do with your decision."

I almost knock over my cup of paint water. "W-what? Of course it didn't." Then I realize what I just admitted to. "I mean, I don't."

"Bullshit, honey, you talk about him nonstop. And now you're gunning for—how did you put it—extra *access*?" She bounces her eyebrows.

"Please shut up," I say on a groan.

But she plows ahead with her teasing anyway. "I guess I should be glad you're dating. I think you'd be more relaxed about work and money if you got laid once in a while."

"I told you it wasn't dating, and nobody is getting laid!"

As she cackles at my pain, my phone rescues me with a chime. It's a text from Austin.

> Hey, I've been thinking about
> you. Still want to get drinks
> soon?

I have to think for a second before I remember who that is. I have his number saved, so—oh yeah, the guy from the coffee shop who liked Delinquent Story. How could I forget? My life's been so crazy lately, all the chaos just shoved the memory of meeting him right out of my brain.

I show my screen to Bianca. "See? This is what a date looks like. Not the weird fantasy you're inventing about me and Dominic."

"It's not just in my head, but hey, whatever you need to believe." Before I can argue back, she asks, "So you're gonna go out with this Austin dude?"

"Sure, why not? He's cute, and he seemed nice." And I really need a distraction right now. A date with Austin will be a welcome dose of normality. *Wouldn't it?*

Bianca snorts. "That doesn't sound very enthusiastic compared to how you talk about—"

"Oh my God, B, enough already. We're just going out, not getting married. I don't have to be crazy about him right off the bat."

"That's fair. I guess I've accepted dates for dumber reasons." She takes a sip of wine.

While the instructor demonstrates the next part of the painting, I text Austin back.

```
I'd  love  to.  How  about  Wednes-
day,  maybe  seven-ish?  You  pick  the
                                place.
```

Only a couple of minutes later, my phone blinks with his very positive response. This man doesn't play games . . .

I add another point next to his name on my mental scoreboard.

• • •

Early on Monday, someone knocks on my cubicle wall. I turn in my chair, expecting Jordan or one of the other interns, only for my heart rate to spike at the sight of Dominic.

Dominic in a dark navy suit looking so fuckable, I have to swallow down a wave of lust.

"Good, you're here," he says. Before I can wonder where else I'd be, he asks, "Do you have a moment to talk?"

"O-oh, of course, please come in."

He's the freaking CEO—I'd make time for him no matter what I was in the middle of. I can only hope this isn't the bad kind of *we need to talk*. I fold my hands attentively in my lap, trying not to wring them.

His dark blue eyes flick back and forth. "I meant privately. In my office."

My nerves flare with a mix of excitement and trepidation. What does he want?

The part of my brain that's been living in the gutter ever since I met Dominic is laser-focused on the prospect of being alone with him. Every other part is panicking over whether I'm about to be fired. But if that were the case, would he seem so strangely on edge?

Well, no matter what's going on here, I have to face it like a professional. I save the document I was working on and get up to follow him.

Dominic leads me through a short maze of halls to his corner office, opens the door, and gestures for me to go first. As I enter, I admire the lavishly appointed room, which boasts a huge, polished cherrywood desk, a matching bookcase packed with volumes of business books, and plush leather chairs around a smoked-glass coffee table for meeting VIPs. It smells like coffee and a hint of Dominic's spicy cedar cologne. I wonder whether the furniture remained from when his father occupied this office, or if Dominic picked it out himself when he took over.

He closes the heavy oak door behind him. All the noise of the bustling workplace beyond it cuts off, leaving us wrapped together in dense silence. "About last Friday night . . ."

My stomach tries to leap out of my body.

CHAPTER NINE

Dominic

I thought dinner with Presley would be manageable, that spending more time with her would somehow numb me to her presence. I hoped coming into work on Monday would be normal and uneventful. Maybe my exhaustion from a weekend with the girls would be enough to keep me tethered to reality.

I thought wrong.

It's like all my senses are on cocaine. Everything is magnified around Presley. The smell of her wafting around me as we made our way toward my office. The sound of her heels on the floor, poking tiny holes into my façade of professionalism. Her slight frame keeps pace with mine from the corner of my eye.

When I first asked her to talk in my office, she froze. But then a soft blush bloomed on her cheeks, and her eyelashes fluttered with a short blink. Was she embarrassed? Nervous?

Regardless, that has to be my favorite of her expressions.

"Of course," she said. I can still hear her voice bouncing needlessly around my head, though nearly half a minute has passed since we stepped into my office and I shut the door.

"About last Friday night . . ."

Presley's lower lip trembles, and her wide blue eyes latch onto mine.

Or maybe that's my favorite.

She's so determined, so earnest, even when everything's about to change between us.

"I think we should talk," I say.

Presley nods, her gaze moving past me to examine my space. Although she's been in my office before, I suppose this is the first chance she's had to really take it in. I kept her pretty preoccupied with assignments her first week, and she tackled them like a pro.

She touches the edge of a frame on the wall that holds an award Aspen Hotels collected the year I began as CEO. She always has this inquisitive look on her face, as if she'll learn everything about me just by scanning the contents of my desk and walls.

"I really do like your office," she says softly, almost to herself.

I pause, letting the silence stretch on. "Thank you."

The space is old-fashioned, but humble. I keep everything in order. While my apartment is littered with chewed-up crayons and miscellaneous toys, not a single thing is out of place here at work.

What's strange is how well she fits in here. Her dark wool skirt and white button-up complement her sharp heels. She's a picture of classic and modern in one petite, hotter-than-hell body. The way she stands in my office, one hand on her hip . . . she looks like she could be running this place herself.

Shit, that's hot.

I try not to acknowledge the way everything below my belt perks up at that thought.

Not fucking now.

"Please, sit," I say, gesturing to the wingback chair that Ollie so often lounges in.

She moves to the chair, placing one delicate hand on the armrest. Her fingernails are trimmed short, filed into a tidy square-ish shape and painted the palest pink.

"Are you going to?" she asks, pausing beside the chair.

"I'd rather stand."

It's easier to hide how jittery I am around this woman when I'm not trying to sit still. Besides, if I sit, there will be a desk between us. Whether I'm conscious of these micro-decisions I'm making or not, I don't want there to be any obstacles between us. Messed up, I know.

"Then I'll stand, too." She rests one hand on the back of the chair. Her knuckles grow white with her grip, but her gaze is steady.

Why is she scared?

"You're not in trouble. The opposite," I say, wanting to reassure her. It must be terrifying to be called into your boss's office first thing Monday morning after the Friday night we shared. "I have a proposition for you."

Her lips quirk up as she considers this.

God, that mouth. I could do bad, bad things to that mouth.

Focus, Dom.

"I need someone reliable. Someone I can count on to be by my side during the next couple of weeks of negotiations. And the appearance that I'm in a steady relationship could help my cause, if I'm being honest. It paints me as dependable, trustworthy."

"I'm not sure I understand," Presley murmurs.

"Outside of working hours, for the next two weeks, I'd like you to pretend to be my . . . plus-one." I almost say girlfriend, but then decide we're not sixteen anymore.

"A two-week arrangement," she says, her brow furrowed. "We would be coworkers, nine to five. And then, after hours, we would be a couple. I understand that much." She pauses, her gaze darting away from mine. "I guess I don't understand what's in it for you. Why now?"

"It's Roger." I cross my arms over my chest. The gray dress shirt I'm wearing pulls tight across my muscles, a sight that apparently doesn't escape her, because I catch her gaze drift over my broad shoulders. I have to bite the inside of my cheek to keep from smiling. "He's a traditional guy, if I'm being polite."

"And if you're not being polite?"

"He's a good ol' boy with no trust or understanding of how business works in the digital age. He does everything in person without any executive help, all by himself. And knowing him, it'll take about two weeks to iron out all the details of our agreement."

"Okay, sure, but I still don't understand. How do I factor in?"

"He likes you," I say, and she scoffs at that, as if I've said something totally absurd. "What? It was obvious. During dinner, he paid more attention to you than he did to me."

"I'm sorry, I—"

"Don't apologize. You're more fun to talk to." There's that blush again. "He's going to expect you at our meetings in the future, as my steady girlfriend."

"Why?" she asks, a bewildered look in her

eyes.

I don't blame her. To me, this is obvious, but to Presley it must seem far-fetched.

I've known Roger since I was a kid. I remember the late-night business dinners at my childhood home. My mother would tuck Teddy and me away for the night and join the men downstairs for a nightcap. That's when the negotiating would begin. My father would lay out the deal and my mother would serve as moderator between the two, pointing out pros and cons, luring Roger in with her intelligent opinion. It was a beautiful game of cat and mouse, and one that worked every time with several clients. It's a formula I'm very familiar with.

Unfortunately, I'm missing a vital element of that formula since I'm a single, twenty-six-year-old CEO.

"Roger is very aware of how young I am to be the head of Aspen Hotels. I need to convince him that I'm serious. We need to. And if he sees me in a committed relationship with a bright, intelligent woman, he'll take me more seriously."

To Roger, I'm still that kid, peeking into his father's study to eavesdrop on the adults. He doesn't see me as much more than a child wandering the halls of his father's grand enterprise.

"By dating?"

"By *pretending* to date. It won't affect your work here at all."

"How could it not?" Presley asks with a little incredulity in her voice. Her cheeks are slightly flushed and her gaze is focused.

I applaud her on her wariness going into an unfamiliar deal. She's handling it just as I would—with an open mind and a touch of good old-fashioned skepticism. *Smart girl.*

"It won't," I say, hoping to reassure her. "It's all laid out in the contract."

"Contract?"

I hand her a single-page document from the top of my desk. It probably wouldn't hold up in a court of law, but it would give us both peace of mind in the meantime.

She scans the page, quickly reading the terms, which are basically what I've already spelled out. It's purely a business arrangement, strictly platonic. All costs will be covered. Meals, travel, and accommodations, if required. And just like the first night she accompanied me, I'll pay her five-hundred dollars for each appearance we make together. Which will probably be several. Roger never comes into the office; it's always dinners or drinks out with him.

"So, what do you say?" I can almost see the thousands of thoughts and uncertainties racing through her beautiful brain. I bet she didn't think this would be part of Aspen's internship program.

I can't say that I did either.

"Can I think about it?" she asks after a beat.

"Of course."

She walks toward the door, and I follow. Together, we pause there, me with my back pressed against the door frame. She's waiting for me to move aside, but I don't.

Why don't I? Because apparently I'm a fucking sadist and need to be close to her despite all the reasons I should keep this professional. Exhibit A, the contract I signed stating that our work would be entirely platonic, both in and out of the office.

Yet here I am, my back glued to the door. Presley is maybe a foot away from me. I haven't been this close to her since I kissed her hand Friday night. I could count her goddamn eyelashes if I wanted to.

"So it is true." Her eyes blaze directly into mine, eradicating any bullshit I may have left to offer.

Fuck. I thought I already addressed this.

"Never mind," she says, shaking her head and looking at the floor.

"No, say it."

Her eyes flash back up to mine, holding me there like a hot hand on my throat. "That you like to pay for it."

My hands curl into fists as if I can hold my faltering calm together with a tight enough grip. Anger bubbles up from the vault of emotions I keep securely locked at all times. I thought I'd been so careful. I never, *ever* disclose this part of my life to anyone who can't be trusted.

Then who the fuck is spreading this rumor? Oliver? I thought I could trust him. Maybe that's not the case, after all.

All burning frustrations immediately subside as Presley takes the smallest step toward me, leaving only inches between us.

"I'm not sleeping with you. Is that clear?" Her voice is quiet, firm, and I find it incredibly sexy.

"I didn't ask you to."

"But is that clear?"

My heart thuds quickly inside my chest. "Yes."

Her eyes are still fixed on mine as if she's searching for a hint of a lie.

There's no lie, Presley. I would never take advantage.

"You don't seem satisfied by that answer."

"I just . . . don't know if it's a good idea," she says softly.

"Why?"

"Because . . ."

Her plump lips form a small pout, and I can't help but stare. Is she wearing any lip color, or are her lips naturally that pink?

"Because why?"

Presley screws her eyes shut in frustration, furrowing her brow. When she opens them, her eyes are like bullets against my useless emotional armor.

"This!" She gestures wildly toward the small space between us, the near-tangible electricity in the air that separates her body from mine.

I fucking knew it. I knew I wasn't the only one.

"You're attracted to me," I say, my voice soft and low. I keep my expression calm and collected, even though I can actually hear my heart pounding through my veins.

Or is that hers?

She stands utterly still, her eyes wide. But slowly, her cheeks grow rosy. Then she draws her bottom lip into her mouth, chewing on it for a moment before letting it pop back out. That little move makes my cock push painfully against the constraints of my pants. I can't tear my eyes away.

"I'm attracted to you, too." I hear myself say it before I process the words falling out of my mouth.

I'm staring at her lips, leaning in.

What am I doing? This meeting is over, Dom.

"Presley—" I'm about to apologize when there's suddenly a soft press of warmth, and I realize Presley is kissing me. Presley, intern extraordinaire and novice escort, has her lips on mine in an almost chaste lip-lock.

Time seems to halt as everything stills.

She places one hand against my chest as if to steady herself. Otherwise, our only point of connection is this kiss.

My eyelids float closed without my permission and I step into her, my hands moving up to cup her warm cheeks in my fingers.

God, she's so small. She's feminine and soft. And it's been so long.

I suck in a sharp inhale, pressing more deeply into her wet lips. She gasps and grips my shirt, clinging for balance. My mind is blank, my world full of Presley's sweet scent and her soft skin and her warm tongue.

I know I should stop. I should control myself

and be the cool, collected CEO.

But with Presley in my arms, there's nothing but fire.

CHAPTER TEN

Presley

I can barely focus on the path back to my desk. My knees are still shaking, my cheeks burn, my lips are still tingling from that kiss. The revelation that Dominic is attracted to me is mind-blowing enough, let alone the idea of pretending we're a couple.

I sit down, open the report I was in the middle of reviewing, and stare at it blankly without absorbing a single word. Instead a rush of thoughts crowd my head. Michael fretting over his school fees. The nerves that twist inside me every time I think about how in the world I'll support both him and I. Then there's everything I could learn about business from observing Dominic and Roger's negotiations. The chance to affect such a significant deal. The possibility of having Dominic's touch, those strong hands and full lips on me again. . . even if it's not written in the contract

I shake my head, uncomfortably warm all over. Am I seriously considering this? No, I can't. Can I?

I'd be lying to an investor. I mean, we wouldn't lie about Aspen's actual business metrics. We'd just be making Dominic look like the kind of stable, mature guy who has a steady girlfriend. It's more of a . . . storytelling technique. Creative advertising. It's done in business models all across the world, the marketing strategies and branding that close deals.

No, that's nonsense—a lie is a lie. On top of that, it would be incredibly unprofessional and inappropriate. I can let myself crash one business dinner, but spending two weeks with the CEO outside of work hours would be unfair to the other interns.

And if we got caught, it wouldn't matter that our relationship was fake. It would look real enough to land us both in deep shit and possibly drag Aspen Hotels' name through the mud. The HR department would freak out, and the PR crisis would be even worse.

My heart is thudding so hard, I'm almost breathless. I flatten my palms against the cool surface of my desk and take a much needed deep breath.

That's when my thoughts take another turn. If we pull this off, everyone will benefit. Me, Michael, Dominic, the entire company. And the idea of spending more time with Dominic is so tempting, for reasons that have nothing to do with what I could learn and everything to do with my attraction to him.

My increasingly tangled thoughts are interrupted when Jordan comes bounding up to my cubicle.

"Hey, Presley. Oliver said our proposal looks great, but some new info came in from the construction company and he wants us to revise our estimate."

"What?" Crap, I didn't process a single word he just said. It's no use—my brain is too full right now. I swivel around to face him. "Sorry, can you repeat that?"

He cocks his head at me. "Is something wrong? You look pale."

"Uh . . . no, I'm just tired," I lie.

He blows a loud sigh of sympathy through his

lips. "Monday mornings, am I right? You want to come grab some coffee while we talk? I was thinking of going to the cafeteria anyway."

"That sounds great, actually." I push out my chair. "Maybe my blood sugar is low."

He flashes me a pleased grin. "There ya go. Snacks solve everything."

Despite my thoughts buzzing around inside my head, I have to chuckle. Seems the absentminded frat bro has an unexpected mother hen side.

In the cafeteria, I take a giant cup of coffee and a blueberry muffin for good measure.

As we find seats, Jordan says, "I had the craziest weekend."

Not crazier than mine, I'll bet. "Yeah?"

As Jordan rambles on about some party he went to, I reply in mostly monosyllables in all the right places, but I can't stop my thoughts from drifting back to Dominic and I pray Jordan doesn't notice, because there's no way in the world I can tell any of the other interns about this.

● ● ●

It's Wednesday evening and I'm supposed to meet Austin in less than an hour, but I'm stuck in neutral. Instead of getting ready, I find myself staring blankly into the mirror with only half my makeup on, trying to figure out what this odd feeling is. It's not bad, exactly, but it's also not good.

Is my intuition trying to warn me away from him? Do I want to bail on this date?

I don't think so. I need a break from all this madness at work—not to mention a cocktail or three—and the prospect of seeing Austin again is a pleasant one. Yet, I'm still strangely reluctant. I still feel an urge to . . . hold something back from him.

I turn and call out, "Hey, B?"

"Yeah?" She sounds like she's in the kitchen.

"Will you come with me?"

A cabinet closes, and soon Bianca pokes her head into the bathroom. "You want me to crash your date?"

I fiddle with my tube of mascara. "Yeah. I just,

I don't know, I suddenly don't feel ready for this to be a serious thing. Does that make sense?"

"Sure, no problem. I'll be your life raft." She pats me on the shoulder. "Scoot over. Where are we going?"

I shift so she can use the mirror, too. "Some bar downtown called Tres Amigos."

"Ooh, your boy toy picked a classy place. Make sure you get one of their mango mojitos." She starts swiping on foundation.

"You've been there? Is the music super loud?" I ask.

"No, Grandma, I promise you can hear yourself think." She pokes out the tip of her tongue at me.

By the time we're on our way, her presence and cheerful teasing have calmed me. A little.

The bar is refined, yet relaxed, with soft golden lighting, hardwood floors, and wide, caramel-colored chairs. Unsurprisingly for a Wednesday, it's also half-empty. As we approach Austin's table, he spots us, and a flicker of disappointment crosses his face.

"Hi, again," I say awkwardly, feeling a bit guilty about upending his plans for the evening. "This is my roommate, Bianca."

But he's graceful about my faux pas. Without hesitation, he smiles and shakes Bianca's hand with a warm, "Nice to meet you."

"You, too. I was curious to finally find out what you looked like," she says with a mischievous quirk to her lips.

"Presley's talked about me? Wow, I'm flattered." He flashes a sheepish grin at me, rubbing the back of his head. "So you're already introducing me to your friends, huh? Wait, forget it . . . that was a bad joke."

Bianca giggles. "Cute," she says, which flusters both me and him.

Austin goes to the bar for us. Per Bianca's recommendation, we order two mango mojitos, and he gets an IPA. Once we're settled with our drinks, he asks, "So, did you two meet at work?"

"Nope, in college," I say. "We were paired up in the dorms as freshmen, and we've been together ever since."

"That's great you've maintained your connection so long. It's too easy to lose touch with old school friends." He sips his beer. "So, what exactly do you do at work?"

Did he not understand me, or is he just clumsy at conversation? Oh well, it's not like my manners have been perfect either.

"A bit of everything," I say with a shrug. "It's an internship, so I'm there to learn—and they also want to test me. But I've only been there a week. So far, most of the work I've done has been in logistics."

"Cool. Can you be more specific?" he asks.

His abruptness catches me by surprise. "Uh, I guess so. Like budget, supply-chain management . . . oh yeah, I've also written a little web copy, I forgot about that."

"You wrote for Aspen's website? So if I went there right now, I'd see your work?"

"Just one page. It's no big deal," I say, feeling a small flush of shy pride. "My boss said he wants to put my programming skills to use on the back end, but that hasn't happened yet."

"Oh, man, for real?" He beams. "You're beautiful, smart, cool, *and* you program, too?"

"Yep. She's pretty much the total package," Bianca says. "You should think about locking her down sooner rather than later."

Austin laughs, and I look into my drink to hide my blush. But instead of answering her, he goes right back to prodding me. "Have you ever done any IT work? Or security?"

This goes on for almost ten more minutes. Every time I reply, Austin instantly fires back another question. As excited as I am to work at Aspen, and as much as I love talking about my job, this is starting to feel less like friendly interest and more like an interrogation.

Finally, I say jokingly, "I feel like I'm at a job interview."

He blinks. "Oh, sorry. I was being awkward, wasn't I? I'm just really curious about the hospitality industry. I've been thinking about changing jobs, and one of my potential leads is a hotel chain. So, about the—"

Bianca leans forward and gives Austin a tight

smile. "I think it's your turn to tell us about yourself. Got any hobbies?"

I wouldn't have said it quite like that, but I've been getting increasingly weirded out by his one-track mind. Honestly, I'm relieved to get off this topic.

After that change of topic, the night becomes much more fun, almost too much fun. The next time I check my phone, it's an hour later.

"We should get going soon," I say, offering him an apologetic look. "Early morning tomorrow. How much were our drinks?"

Austin spreads his palms with a smile. "Don't worry about it. They're on me tonight."

"Oh . . . are you sure?" When he nods, I say, "Thank you."

"Have a good night." He shakes Bianca's hand again and gives me a hug. No kiss, no romantic comments. We might as well just be friends.

I feel oddly relieved, then frustrated with myself. He's a perfectly decent guy—why can't I want him, too? Why does my body insist upon reacting only to the man who's such a bad idea in so many ways?

When Bianca and I get home, we wash off our makeup and say good night. She turns out the lights. I lie down on the couch and wriggle around, trying to get comfortable. But half an hour later, I'm still wide awake, Dominic and his shocking proposal swirling through my head.

Sure, I could justify this financially, but what about ethically? And even if I'm not doing anything wrong, what would happen to my career if anyone found out? How safe would my secret be?

On the other hand, Michael needs this money ASAP. And it might be nice to eat something other than instant ramen for the next three months. If things go well, I could even put down a deposit on my own apartment. Bianca wouldn't have to put up with my couch-surfing anymore—she always insists that it's fine, but I'm sure she'd prefer privacy. My aching back also likes the sound of a real bed. Plus, I wouldn't have to live out of a suitcase . . .

With a harried grunt, I flip on the end table lamp and dig through said suitcase for my tarot deck. I concentrate on my question about my future as I shuffle, draw a card, and set it face down on the coffee table. Then I draw four cards, two on each side of the first. Finally, beneath the rest of the spread, I lay down one card for advice.

I flip over the first card. My current situation is . . . the Five of Coins. I snort. No crap, I was already painfully aware of my financial difficulties.

The second and third cards, representing sticking to my current path, are the Hanged Man and the Ten of Wands. Neither card holds much good news. They represent someone struggling under an exhausting burden, taking too much responsibility onto my shoulders. While I'm not afraid of hard work, I hesitate at this card's strong hint that overextending myself might result in nothing but pointless pain.

The next two cards are totally bizarre. The Lovers and the Three of Swords. Passion and desire. But the latter card implies strong emotions, too . . . specifically, heartbreak and betrayal. *Terrific*.

I leave them for now and move on to the last card. What advice will the tarot offer me? I flip it over and snort when the Fool is revealed.

Maybe I've been overthinking this. Sometimes we have to leave the comfortable path to find the best solution to a problem.

The worst that could happen probably isn't the nightmare that my runaway anxiety is conjuring, but it's still pretty damn bad. There aren't many cards more dire than the Three of Swords. And the Lovers is too unclear to be of any real comfort.

I'm used to pushing myself. I know how to bust my ass, focus, and sacrifice. It's what I'm good it, and has gotten me this far in life.

I rub my thumb over the three figures on the Lovers card. I shouldn't let myself get caught up in foolish, schoolgirl fantasies about the sexy and intense Dominic Aspen. But it's almost impossible not to. Remembering the way he kissed me in his office floods my blood with something hot and unspoken. Dirty fantasies flash through my brain—his long eyelashes fluttering closed as he gave himself over to the kiss—the warmth of his tongue touching mine for the first time—the scent of leather and cedar filling all my senses. A low ache forms between my legs and I huff out a sigh.

Frustrated, I push my fingers through my hair. I don't freaking know—I'm too tired and confused and conflicted to think straight right now. I put the cards away, turn off the lamp, and try again to sleep.

I don't remember drifting off. But I must have, because I dream of Dominic's kiss.

CHAPTER ELEVEN

Dominic

I can tell Fran's in a mood today before she even opens her mouth.

"Why haven't I seen you with a woman lately?" she asks, hanging up her coat in the front hall closet.

It's a great fucking question, but I don't have time for this. It's Friday morning, and I have to leave in less than five minutes to head to the office.

I bring my mug of coffee to my lips, taking a sip in order to buy myself some time. She's great with my kids and I love her, but damn, is she nosy.

"Did you hear me?" she asks, reaching for the teakettle, and turns the heat on high to make herself a cup of tea.

I'm starting to regret giving her a key. I'd like a little warning before I get scolded.

"Maybe I'm not into women."

"Then why haven't I seen you with a man?" she asks without missing a beat.

I roll my eyes, tightening my tie around my throat as I stand up from the table. *Damn.* I rub my temples. I haven't had near enough caffeine for this yet.

"It's been three years, Dom," Fran says, as if I needed reminding.

Her tone is maternal, low and soft, but her words still sting. My hand clenches around the drawer handle for a moment before I open it and pluck a spoon from inside.

Goddamn, Francine. Cut me some slack.

"I'm not looking for anything serious," I say, keeping my tone casual and light. I learned that lesson when I very seriously gave my heart to a woman who saw no issue with crushing it under the heel of her boot.

"That's absurd." Fran sighs and reaches for

a mug in the cabinet before fixing her tea. "I just think you should think about your daughters."

"I am thinking about my daughters," I respond coolly. "I'm *only* thinking about them." They get all of my free time and attention without having to share me with someone else.

I place my yogurt and spoon into the side pocket of my laptop bag and head for the door. "I'll be home late tonight," I call out, and hear Fran make a disgruntled noise.

Fantastic. As if I don't have enough to worry about.

The week has flown by, and tonight I have plans to meet with Roger to discuss the stipulations of our agreement. He's expecting Presley to be on my arm. Unfortunately, she hasn't committed to our little agreement yet. Instead, she's been avoiding me, spending all her time in front of her computer or surrounded by the other three interns.

When I arrive at the office, I intend to confront Presley, but I'm stopped in the hall by my finance director and spend nearly an hour in an impromptu meeting about next quarter's earnings. After that, I have two meetings back to back, one with a city council member, and then my staff meeting. Oliver sticks around after the meeting, briefing me on the beefed-up cyber security plans we were forced to create after a system breach last year.

"Everything looks good," I tell him, but I'm distracted, and I'm pretty sure Oliver knows why.

By the time I'm through, I spot Presley chatting casually with Jordan at the coffee bar. He's telling her some story about his evening, showing off, trying to be funny. Presley doesn't seem to mind at all. She laughs softly into her coffee, her body language relaxed and open. She seems to like him.

What a prick.

I take a deep breath. Now isn't the time to get aggravated with my employees—especially not some immature frat boy. This has to be resolved . . . now.

Presley had the whole week to come to a decision. I've given her the space she wanted and never even mentioned our unfinished business during our brief, almost nonexistent exchanges. It doesn't matter that if I concentrate, I can still feel the warmth of her face against my palms and taste the sweetness of her lips on my tongue.

I clear my throat. "Can I have everyone's attention?"

The white noise of the office softens to a low hum as hands still at keyboards and conversations halt in mid-sentence. Everyone's attention turns my way.

"Thank you all for a great week. Interns, especially, we're very impressed and grateful for your dedication. Take the rest of the day off. Enjoy the weekend."

My employees look a little stunned, unaccustomed to half days. Jordan fist-bumps Presley, who maneuvers through the motion with a little difficulty, nearly spilling her coffee.

"Except for you, Presley. I need to speak with you in my office."

The office becomes dead silent then, quieter than I've ever heard it during work hours.

Presley's complexion turns pale right before her cheeks grow bright pink. But she isn't embarrassed or nervous, I realize. She looks fucking furious.

Jordan looks at her, then at me, and then back

at her. "See you Monday, Pres," he says, feigning a casual tone, but she won't tear her gaze away from me long enough to even give him a convincing good-bye.

"Come with me."

Presley is hot on my trail. I can practically feel her bursting with frustration, and I can relate to that sensation. Although, my frustration is of an entirely different brand. She's got me in her crosshairs before the door even closes.

"You can't do that. Not in front of everyone. What will people think?"

"First, I don't care what they think. They report to me, not the other way around. And second, they'll probably assume we have business to settle, which we do."

She's quiet for a moment, before looking down at her shoes. "I just don't want people thinking that we're involved somehow."

"Involved?" I ask.

"Sleeping together," she says.

I study her for a moment. She's so determined.

So breathtakingly put together. "But we're not sleeping together."

"I know! But—" Presley cuts herself off, pressing her fingers to her temples. She takes a breath, her eyes closed, calming herself. "I just don't want people talking."

When she opens her eyes, I'm struck by her expression. It's as if she's trying to decide whether to believe me.

I want her to know that I'm genuinely sorry for putting her in an uncomfortable situation. I want her to feel safe with me. I would have never asked her to stay behind in front of the staff if this had occurred to me.

But she's right. She's a woman, a beautiful young woman, and I'm a man, and people talk. Unfortunately. That's just a sad fact of business.

"I'm sorry. That didn't occur to me. It won't happen again."

Her expression softens, and I want to touch her. My fingers are tucking a loose strand of hair behind her ear before I have time to decide whether I should cross that line. She seems surprised, but she doesn't move away or break eye contact with me.

Interesting.

"Are you coming with me tonight? I've been more than patient."

"I know. And yes."

"Yes, what?"

"I'll come. I'll be there for the dinner."

"Thank you," I say emphatically, offering her my hand so we can shake on our deal.

A smile broadens across her pretty face, and I can't help but smile back in return. I let my thumb caress her wrist before letting go.

"You can sign at my desk," I say, gesturing to the contract set neatly upon its surface.

Her heels click as she walks over and picks up the pen. Even from a few feet away, I can see that her signature is beautiful—not too loopy, sharp and simple.

"I'll pick you up at five thirty. We're expected at six."

"Do you have a preference for what I wear?"

"I trust your instinct."

"Wow, a compliment." Presley smirks.

The corner of my own mouth quirks as I walk her toward the door. "You'll be getting plenty of those tonight, so get used to it."

"I'll do my best," she says with a cheeky grin.

"See you at five thirty."

"See you then."

The door clicks closed behind her, and just like that, everything is in motion.

• • •

I knew I'd be worthless at work for the next few hours with my mind racing like it is. Shortly after Presley left, I also took off for the day. I have to be mentally prepared for anything Roger throws at me tonight. But first, a little recharge.

I ease open the door to my daughters' room. It's naptime, so they're usually tucked in around this time, but their beds are empty.

Where are they?

"They're in your bed," comes a voice from less than a foot away, and I nearly jump out of my goddamn skin.

"Jesus, Fran!" How does a woman who wears fucking New Balance shoes sneak up on me so easily?

"You'll be gone till late again?"

"Yes," I say, averting my gaze. *I really can't handle any more judgment from you.*

"All right," she says, squeezing my arm. "Go spend some time with your little ones before you leave."

I nod, turning down the hall toward my own room. The girls are curled up together on top of the duvet, two little cherubs holding hands.

Smiling, I kick off my shoes and climb in between them, lifting Emilia gently to give myself some space to lie down. She sleeps like the dead, so I have no worries of waking her. I lower myself onto the bed, tangling my fingers in Lacey's curls and tucking Emilia against my chest. I listen to the whispers of their breathing—so soft, so steady.

I consider for a moment just staying like this

for the rest of the afternoon. I could wake them up, take them out for ice cream, and put on one of our favorite movies. We could all snuggle close on the couch. I can almost hear the sound of Emilia sucking on her thumb and feel the tangles of Lacey's hair as I try to unknot them before bed.

Maybe another time.

After a little while, I get up, careful not to wake them. My shoeless feet pad across the floor toward the bathroom. In a few minutes, I'm standing under the scalding downpour of my shower, letting the water burn away any hesitation I have about tonight.

There was no chance of sneaking out before the girls woke up. When I'm clean and dressed, I find them sitting up in my bed, both reaching for me with sleepy eyes and adorable yawns. I pick one up in each arm and they relax into my chest. I'm not always going to be able to hold them like this, so I do it as often as I can.

I carry them to my dresser and plop Lacey on top. Emilia is still waking up, her warm little nose nestled in the crook of my dress shirt collar. This is a game we've played before, so Lacey looks expectantly at the first small drawer. I slide it open, revealing all the cuff links I've acquired over the years. A gold pair from graduation. Two pairs gifted to me by my mother a long time ago. A silver pair I inherited from Teddy.

Emilia prefers the smaller, prettier ones, the ones my mother gave me. Lacey's the one choosing this time, though.

"Bis!" she blurts, one fat little finger pointing at Teddy's silver cuff links with the square crowning. She jabbers some more, and I laugh at her gibberish. They're a little gaudy for my taste, but the lady insists.

I snap the cuff links into place. *Just like if Teddy were coming with me.*

"Now, which tie?"

• • •

As expected, Presley's presence is a game changer. Roger is nearly red in the face with laughter, eating up every second of this woman's attention. At first, I thought he was merely excited to have the attention of a younger woman. But now I'm fairly convinced that he genuinely likes her as a person.

As he should.

Presley flashes me a pretty smile, and my heart clenches like it did when she first walked out of her apartment earlier this evening.

"Aren't you cold?" I asked as she slid into the passenger seat of my Porsche.

She froze momentarily, her hands hovering over the seat belt and door handle. "Should I change? Too much skin?"

"No, you look great. And if you get cold, I'll give you my coat."

"Oh, right. Good detail."

I swallowed, looking away. For a moment, I'd forgotten that this was all an elaborate, staged scheme of ours. I was just going to give her my coat to warm her, not to make things look more convincing. "Devil's in the details."

We then fell into a comfortable silence. The Seattle streetlights zipped by.

"I was expecting a limo," she said, out of the blue.

"Oh, was this not extravagant enough for you?" I smirked.

"Jesus, no! This is your car?"

"It is."

I wasn't about to pull up with the SUV and its car seats nestled into the back row. No, this version of me drives a Porsche, a recent model with plenty of horsepower. I may be a single dad, but I can still have a bachelor's sports car.

"I don't have a car," she said matter-of-factly.

"You don't need one in the city."

"So, why do you have one?"

"Because I can afford it," I said with a grin, and she smiled back at me with a short laugh.

And that was how our car ride went. Playful. Comfortable. Fun.

• • •

So far, dinner is meeting every one of my expectations. The only bump in the road is that Roger refuses to talk business. The fat old bastard.

"There's always time for office talk," he says, brushing aside my second attempt at focusing. "I'm enjoying this young lady's company."

Presley gives me a knowing smile and turns back to Roger. "It's as if he thinks we can't do both," she says, pretending to be appalled.

Roger practically roars with laughter.

I shrug with as much of a charismatic smile as I can offer. *She's got me.*

"You know what," Roger says hoarsely, after he's recovered. "You two should come to the waterfront."

"The what?" Presley asks.

"It's my weekend home, right on the Sound. A couple of hours from here. Monica and I are going tomorrow morning. You should join us."

In unison, Presley says, "Oh no, we couldn't—" right as I say, "We'd love to." She turns to me with a desperate look in her eyes.

Reaching under the table, I find her hand resting on her knee. I give it a reassuring squeeze as if to say, *We'll talk about it later.*

"That's fucking fantastic," Roger says, raising his glass. "To spontaneity!"

"To spontaneity."

With dinner finally done, Presley walks several paces ahead of me, purposely keeping her distance as we head to the car. She didn't even give me a chance to ask the valet to bring it around for us. After jogging to catch up with her, I grab her hand, and she snatches it back as if I've burned her.

"You keep doing that," she says.

"Doing what?"

"Touching me."

"I'm sorry." The apology is reflexive. "I won't do it again."

"It's fine," she says, backpedaling.

"No, it's not. I won't do it again without your permission."

She accepts that easier than she did my last apology. We get to the car, but Presley leans against the door to face me before I can unlock it for her.

"I don't want to go to Roger's place."

"Why not?"

"It's a whole weekend. That's a lot more involved than one dinner every now and then."

"It's a lot to ask, I know."

"Yes, it is." Her cheeks are pink, and her arms are crossed against her chest as if she's cold. Seattle is always a little chilly at night, no matter the season.

"Would you like my jacket?"

She shakes her head, lips pressing into a line.

"Let's get in the car." I reach around her to put my hand on the door handle. When she doesn't move, I let my hand drop away, determined to keep my promise not to touch her.

"I need you," I hear myself saying. "Presley, I need your help."

A small crease forms between her eyebrows, but she's staring at my lips again, giving me that look she gave me in my office on Monday. The look I wasn't sure I was ever going to see again—hooded eyes, wet lips, and a faint blush. And it's pulling me in. Big fucking time.

It doesn't matter that I'm the boss and she's my employee. Because right now? I've never been more aware of the fact that I'm a man, and she's a woman.

I shrug off my coat and place it around her shoulders, thinking how tiny she looks wearing my large coat on her slight frame.

"You're cold. Please wear it." I step into her, as close as I can without pinning her against the car, then softly brush her jawline with my knuckles, my gaze fixed on her pink lips.

Looking deeply into her eyes, I ask a silent question. *May I?*

She nods, and my heart stops.

I press a kiss to her mouth, intending for it to be slow, chaste. But Presley's lips open against mine, and I'm shot back in time to our kiss in my office, reliving that first touch of her tongue.

But this kiss is even more desperate and wild. She lets out a soft moan, lifting on her toes to get closer, her fingers curling into my jacket. I couldn't pull away from her if I wanted to. And I sure as hell don't want to.

My hands skim down her waist as she rakes her teeth gently against my lower lip.

God, I want her.

When we break apart, I struggle to find my voice.

"Please come?"

"Okay," she agrees, breathlessly.

CHAPTER TWELVE

Presley

Sliding into the buttery-soft leather seat the next morning, I huff out a sigh. It took some convincing, but in the end, Dominic won, and I agreed to accompany him to Roger's waterfront home on the condition that it was only for one night.

Dominic agreed easily with my terms, and so here we are, his shiny black limo parked at the curb in front of my building. He chats with the chauffeur as my overnight bag is placed in the trunk, and then he slides in beside me.

As the driver pulls back into traffic, Dominic turns to me, his expression serious. "Are you okay?"

I nod and stuff my phone into my purse. "I'm fine."

He's a puzzle I'm still trying to solve. A CEO and billionaire who sometimes acts every inch the dominating powerhouse the media makes him out to be. And then other times, my favorite times, he's softer somehow, transforming into a twenty-something single guy you'd meet at the corner bar for a beer and a slice of pizza. Part of the fun on these little excursions, I'm coming to realize, is that I never quite know which version of him I'm going to get.

The breathless feeling in my chest grows with each of his worried glances. What will happen later? What do I want to happen later?

We head toward the highway, and Dominic presses a button to raise the privacy screen, separating us from the driver.

He runs one hand over the back of his neck, looking a little uncertain. "I've been thinking . . . we have some work to do. If Roger's going to believe we're a couple, we need to get our stories straight. Make it look like we know each other well."

"Makes sense," I reply, nodding. "Well, we've got two hours to kill right now. Let's talk."

I smooth my dark-washed jeans over my thighs

and feel a little thrill at the way his gaze flicks down for a second. I'm dressed casually in jeans, a bright red sweater, and tall boots. I have a black cocktail dress packed into my overnight bag since I'm not sure what to expect later or how formal things will be.

"Perfect. You go first." His mouth twitches in a small smirk. "And nothing professional, I already know all that."

I think for a minute, acutely aware of his focus on me. I don't leave much room in my life for hobbies, friends, or anything else besides work. Unearthing ugly family history seems too intimate for this stage. And, oh God, the idea of admitting my embarrassing lack of a love life . . . Yeah, no, that won't be happening.

"Well," I say slowly, "I live with my best friend, Bianca. I like to read." I hesitate. "And you're probably going to laugh at this, but my grandma taught me to read tarot cards, and it's still a hobby of mine."

"I won't laugh. But I admit, I didn't expect that from someone so left-brained." He leans back, setting his ankle on his opposite knee. "Can you predict my future?"

Although his light tone is amused, it's not derisive, and I'm relieved that he isn't judging my little hobby.

"That's not quite how it works. It's more like a decision-making tool—at least, that's how I use it. To guide you toward a path when you're unsure."

He considers this. "Interesting. So you already know the answer deep down, and the cards are just a tool you use to dig for it."

"Exactly." Feeling bolder now, I say, "Okay, it's your turn now. Tell me something special about yourself. Something secret." I'm excited to be learning more about the Dominic that people in the office don't get to see.

He pauses, his chin resting on his hand while he considers my question. Then he says, "I was a super nerd until I hit puberty."

I laugh in delight. "Oh, really? Tell me more." I scoot a little closer, eager to hear more.

"Ha, no thanks. I think I'll pass on those details."

"Come on, don't be like that. I like hearing about the things no one else knows."

"You mean my flaws?" He shrugs. "I have loads of them."

"Doesn't seem like it from where I'm sitting." Which is currently almost touching him.

"Trust me." He points to himself. "Riddled with shortcomings."

I can't help but chuckle. The man is in a ten-thousand-dollar suit, wearing custom-made cuff links and a vintage Rolex, and he's also self-deprecating. I think I just fell a little harder.

"So, what's the big secret, then?" I ask. "The thing you don't want people to know?"

He looks lost in thought, his gaze drifting to the window for a moment while he thinks. And when he speaks, his tone is cooler. "I'm really particular about my coffee."

I raise my brows. "Your coffee."

"I'm a coffee snob." He shrugs.

I roll my eyes. "That's it? That's the huge reveal? The extent of your big, dirty secret?"

Dominic smirks again. "For now. Why? What about you? Any skeletons in the closet I should know about?"

I consider his question. It's insane. And hilarious. Does he really expect me to answer?

"Maybe?" I say, my voice betraying me. My lack of confidence is obvious.

He chuckles. "Spill it, intern."

"Intern?" I exhale sharply and place a hand over my heart in mock outrage. But the secret truth is that I like his silly nickname. I've felt like anything but an intern lately. Everything has felt so intense and real.

"I'm sorry," Dominic says, his voice turning serious. "To be honest, you're nothing like any intern I've ever met before. You're . . ."

When he pauses, I find myself leaning forward, eager to hear what he's going to say.

"Smart. No . . ." His eyebrows scrunch together. "You're brilliant. Your SAT scores, your GPA . . ." He waves a hand in the air. "Never mind. You're just . . . different. And very driven."

"Thank you." I smile and duck my head, but there's no need to be modest. I graduated college at the top of my class with a 4.0 average. I've had multiple internships at major corporations. Bianca's right—I'm pretty much a badass. It's just nice to know Dominic sees me that way, instead of just a pretty face.

A smirk pulls at the corner of his mouth. "You know," he says, his deep voice lingering over the words in a way that's decidedly sexy, "to pull this weekend off, we also need to be comfortable with touching each other."

My eyebrows lift. "Touching each other?"

He nods. "Kissing. Hand-holding. That type of thing," he says way too innocently.

"I see." My voice is tight, and too soft.

"We could practice that now." His mouth twitches with a smile again.

I laugh. "Is that so?"

I'm trying to keep my tone light and teasing, but my heart is hammering a million miles a minute, and butterflies have erupted inside my stomach.

I slide a fraction closer to him and lift my chin, and then his hot mouth is on mine.

My lips part and Dominic's skilled tongue touches mine, leaving me almost dizzy. We've kissed before, but it's never been like this. This fiery, this intense. His hand moves to my jaw, my neck, his hold gentle but thrillingly strong. I nip at his lower lip, earning a rough growl of approval that makes my inner muscles clench.

His hand slides over my neck and collarbone, caressing closer and closer to my chest. I moan into his mouth in anticipation—only for him to avoid touching my breast as his hand skims down my side. After drawing a tingling trail down my waist, my hip, his hand settles firmly on my lower back.

My whimper of disappointment breaks into a squeak when he pulls me to straddle his lap.

"Intern, I'm going to enjoy taking my time with you," he murmurs near my ear, raising goose bumps all the way down my spine.

• • •

Two hours later, the car rolls to a stop.

I hurry to make myself presentable, but while I can fix my lipstick, there's not much I can do about how pink my cheeks are. Dominic straightens his tie and smooths his hair, rumpled from me running my fingers through it.

How is he so cool and collected when I'm about to explode from need? But no, when I look closer, his eyes glitter with hunger, and I feel a rush of horny satisfaction that I've incited such a response from him.

Our chauffeur opens the door and extends a hand to help us out. If he suspects we spent the entire trip flirting and kissing, he doesn't betray a hint of it.

A man in a suit has already emerged from the house to greet us. When he starts unloading the trunk, I automatically move to help, only for him to wave me off with a smile.

"It's all right, miss. I'll handle your bags."

With an amused sparkle in his eyes, Dominic offers me his hand. We stroll arm in arm up the winding flagstone path. The impressive house ahead of us, overlooking the breeze-ruffled water, is white with a slate roof and navy trim. The property extends to the shoreline, where a large sailboat floats near a dock, bobbing in the tide. It's beautiful here. Utterly serene. Too bad I feel anything but relaxed.

Roger appears at the front door, beaming. He's dressed casually in khakis and a polo shirt. "I'm so glad you two could make it. This is my favorite spot to be on the weekend." He gives a hearty handshake to first me, then Dominic.

"I can see why," Dominic answers, releasing his hand.

"I'll show you to your room."

Room. Singular, not plural. My stomach flips.

Of course. If we're supposed to be in a serious relationship, he'd assume we share a bed. I repress a gulp, not knowing if I'm excited or nervous. Maybe it's a bit of both. As we follow Roger through the house, he points out different features. There's a library and a home theater filled with half a dozen leather recliners.

He pauses in front of a picture window that overlooks the water. "I'm sorry to say Monica couldn't make it this weekend. But I think we'll still have fun." He winks and continues on, while I try to reset my expectations about what I thought would be a couples' weekend.

Roger shows us down the hall to a stylish suite that looks half the size of Bianca's entire apartment, then says, "Dinner will be ready soon. If you'd like to freshen up, please do, and then join us for some cocktails."

"Us?" I ask.

"In Monica's absence, I invited a few friends of mine. When you're ready, I'll introduce you."

When Roger and Dominic exit the bedroom, I change into my black dress and matching heels, grateful that I brought something more formal. After I brush my hair and touch up my makeup, I emerge to find Dominic waiting in the hall. I'm grateful he didn't follow Roger off into the house somewhere and abandon me.

His gaze skims the length of me, but he's quiet.

"Is this okay?" I ask, my stomach tightening.

"You look perfect."

His words hit me square in the chest as he takes

my hand to lead me down the hall. But then, I remind myself, he only means I look perfect for playing the part of the serious girlfriend of the young playboy CEO. This is a role I'm being paid handsomely for, and I'll play it well. That's all.

As we head farther into the beautifully appointed home, we hear voices. I glance at Dominic, uncertain. His expression is neutral in a way that seems purposely diplomatic. Maybe I'm not the only one who isn't thrilled with this development. It's Roger's house, he's entitled to invite whomever he wants . . . but I don't like the unpredictability of adding extra people into the mix, and I'm not sure Dominic does either.

Dominic leads us to a living area dominated by a stone fireplace, where Roger and two gray-haired men sit in leather armchairs drinking cocktails from crystal tumblers.

"Gentlemen, these are the kids I told you about earlier," Roger says when he spots us approaching. "Dominic, Presley, this is Albert and Ernest."

He points at each man as he mentions their names, and they incline their heads at us, raising their glasses.

"Now," he says, "what'll it be? I can whip up anything you want, so long as it's a Negroni." He winks at me.

I chuckle and offer to help, but Roger waves me off, telling me to relax and make myself comfortable.

If only that were possible. This might be a vacation house, but I'm definitely on work time. I think…

I'm standing next to the hottest man on the planet, who also happens to be my boss. I'm pretending to be his girlfriend and will be sharing a bed with him tonight. There's no part of this situation that's even remotely comfortable.

While we sip our cocktails, I learn that Albert is a hedge fund manager, and Ernest is the vice president of a petroleum exploration company. Now I feel even more out of my element. I'm a freaking unpaid intern, and very aware of that fact as I listen to them speak. I'm relieved when the man who took our bags reappears to announce that dinner is served.

The chef serves a sumptuous meal of red snapper, arugula salad with pine nuts, and pomegranate parfait. It all looks delicious. So much better than my usual dinner of something overcooked in the microwave.

"My doctor said I had to go on that Mediterranean diet," Roger says, patting his paunch. "I'm enjoying it more than I thought I would, to be honest."

As dinner goes on, I start to relax. Their conversation topics—management, financial strategy, cyber security issues, rumors about competitors—prove easy for me to jump into, even if I'm sometimes limited to just asking questions. And Dominic is an inspiring sight, chatting conversationally with a polished flair, totally in his element.

He has this whole brooding spoiled rich boy vibe that should be infuriating. Instead it's so damn endearing. Watching the way he carries himself, hearing him converse about complex topics so easily—you instantly know he was raised attending all the best boarding schools money could buy. Not only that, if you look closely, you can also tell he was denied the warm affections of his parents from an age that was far too tender. I want to squeeze him in a hug as inappropriate as that seems. Then again that could just be the alcohol I've had going to my head.

When our plates have been cleared, Roger herds everyone to his study and pours us each a brandy, but I refuse as politely as I can. I'm already tipsy and still haven't finished my glass of imported wine from dessert.

Nobody is talking about business anymore; they've all moved on to sports, politics, their kids and grandkids, anecdotes about old friends. After about half an hour of smiling and nodding, I excuse myself to the balcony for some fresh air.

Wineglass in hand, I lean against the railing, admiring the nighttime view. Moonlight silvers the lawn and scatters, glittering, over the black mirror of the water. Wind rustles the shadowed trees below, and I shiver a little.

"Here." Dominic drapes his suit jacket over my shoulders. The men chatting inside are loud enough, I hadn't heard him approach.

"Oh, thank you." I snuggle into his jacket, enjoying his lingering warmth. Hugging it around me, I inhale the woodsy, masculine scent of his cologne.

"That dress is hardly made for a cool summer night," he says. "But I can't deny it looks incredible on you."

I decide not to tell him I had to borrow it from Bianca. "You look great, too."

He looks better than great . . . in fact, he looks downright edible. I want to press close to him, continue what we started in the limo, but I'm too aware of the gaggle of old men laughing and drinking on the other side of the window.

"How do you think we're doing so far?" I ask, indicating the others with a tilt of my head.

"I was just about to ask you the same thing." Dominic glances back at them. "My impression is pretty positive."

"Mine, too. Roger seems happy."

"And it's all thanks to you," he says.

My cheeks warm. "Me? But you . . ." *Fit in with them.*

Dominic moves so smoothly among these men, it's easy to forget he's only a few years older than me. I've been second-guessing myself all night, constantly feeling moments away from tripping over my own tongue.

"You're so much more natural with them," I say instead. After all, he was born to this high-powered lifestyle.

Dominic chuckles. "You haven't seen how Roger behaves when it's only me. Trust me, he's enthralled with you. That's the only reason why he's started giving me a fair chance." He rests his arm around my waist, and its heat burns right through the thin dress fabric to my skin. "And we're more alike than you think, Presley. You have no reason to feel out of place."

"Are you saying I'm a—how'd you put it—a 'super nerd?' Is that what's happening here?" I arch my brows at him playfully.

"No, uh, of course not." He's rambling, and I've never heard Dominic ramble. In fact, I've never heard him be anything less than one-hundred-percent confident and calculated.

My lips lift in a smile. I like this cautious, flirty side to him. I like it enough to dare teasing him more.

"Speaking of nerds, that reminds me. In the limo, I told you several things about myself, but you only told me one. I don't think that's fair."

"And you want to collect what I owe?" he asks, a husky note to his voice that makes my insides tighten. "What are you going to do about it?"

"I'll start by asking nicely. If that doesn't work . . . we'll see." I lean closer to him. "So, what's your story? Are you more than just a hot CEO?"

His mouth twitches in a smile. I just called him hot, and while he doesn't comment on it, he's clearly tucking that tidbit away. But I have no regrets. The man is hot as fuck. His confidence alone is off the charts, and the looks to go with that level of charisma take everything to another level.

"Honestly, I love it. And I hate it at the same time."

"What do you love about it?"

"Being the person everyone looks to when shit is going wrong. I pride myself on staying calm under pressure."

He's right. Dominic is like a lighthouse in a stormy sea. Everyone looks to him for direction.

He's so steady and certain. It lends him a reassuring presence.

"And what do you hate about it?" I imagine he's going to say the hours or the high expectations or the public scrutiny involved in pleasing stockholders. But he surprises me yet again.

"It was supposed to be Teddy's job." His eyes are stormy and dark, and I can't read his expression at all.

"Teddy?"

"My brother, my father's protégé. He was waiting his whole life for this."

The older brother who died young. I came across an article about him online once, and now I recall the details—it was a drunk-driving accident.

Suddenly, I ache for Dominic. It's obvious that his brother's death left a lasting hole in his heart, and that he harbors some guilt about taking over the company when it was always supposed to go to his older brother.

Overcome with a sudden wave of emotion, I reach over and squeeze his hand. "Do you miss him?" I ask quietly. I know I'd never get over it if anything ever happened to Michael.

"Sometimes." Dominic's voice is restrained. He blows out a sigh. "But then I get so fucking mad at him that he drove drunk that night, rather than call for a car, that I don't miss him at all."

"That's not true. Don't say that. You can be mad, but don't say that."

His eyes meet mine, and I'm startled by their beauty. Deep blue with flecks of steely gray. They're stunning.

"I have a younger brother. Michael," I say.

He nods in understanding. "Are you close?"

"Very. He's a dancer . . . wants to go into ballet. My dad pretty much disowned him, and since my mom died, I'm all he has."

Dominic leans in, his face tilting to mine. "He's lucky to have you," he says softly.

His breath just barely tickles my lips, and my heart skips in anticipation. He moves closer . . .

Until loud ringing breaks the evening stillness. Dominic pulls back, taking his phone from his jacket pocket. I try not to glare at the damn thing for interrupting.

At the sight of the screen, he widens his eyes for a second before he schools his features. "Excuse me—it's a private call," he murmurs.

And before I can ask what's going on, he's already walking briskly inside, leaving me alone and confused on the balcony.

What was *that* all about? I thought we were opening up to each other, and suddenly he yanked that controlled mask over his face and rushed off. I've never seen Dominic so rattled. It was almost like . . . he got caught in a secret.

Work wouldn't call him at this hour. Maybe family would, but I doubt he'd act that way if that were the case. Given everything I've learned about his life, I'd assumed he was single, but could he actually be in a relationship? Unhappily married? I sure as hell hope not, considering I spent almost two hours making out with him today.

The idea that I might be "the other woman" claws at my stomach. I want answers, right freaking now, and all the alcohol I've had tonight gives me liquid courage.

I drain the last drops of wine from my glass and strike out in the direction he just headed, determined to confront him.

A little niggling in the back of my alcohol-induced brain reminds me that the answers I get may not be the answers I want.

CHAPTER THIRTEEN

Dominic

"Good night. I love you."

I haven't even hung up my phone before Presley bursts into the bedroom where I came to have a little privacy. Every evening, Emilia and Lacey need a good-night from Daddy before they can settle into bed. Fran started this ritual, and it's one that I look forward to . . . I just wish the timing of it had been better. I didn't want to leave Presley alone on the balcony after our moment, but there was no choice.

"Who was that?" Presley's cheeks are stained pink.

Standing next to the bed, I pocket my phone. "I was just about to rejoin you on the balcony."

She stands her ground, and I take a step closer.

"It's really not your business," I say, keeping my tone even.

"Are you seeing someone else?"

Fuck, she's even hotter when she's angry. "I'm not seeing anyone."

"Then who were you talking to?"

I swallow. "I can't tell you that."

"Why not?" she asks, her hands falling to her sides. She seems genuinely perplexed. But there's no way in hell I'm telling her I was on the phone with my two toddlers.

"It's not personal, Presley. There are very few people who know about my private life. I can count them on one hand. I like to keep it that way. The phone call was a family matter."

Presley opens her mouth to object and then snaps it shut. She seems somewhat saddened by what I've said; the color drains from her cheeks and her gaze drops to the floor at her feet. "A family matter," she repeats.

Could I have hurt her feelings?

"Trust me," I say, not entirely sure what I mean. "It has no bearing on our arrangement." I take a step toward her, and her eyes flash up to mine.

"Right," she says, her voice cracking under the guise of strength. "Just because we're sharing a bed doesn't mean that we're sharing our lives."

Sharing a bed? Why didn't it occur to me that there was only one bed? Or that we'd be spending the night in it together? Well, that's going to be one hell of a cock tease, complete with my least-favorite bedtime story ever, *Goodnight Hard-On.*

"Well, you're welcome to the floor, if you'd prefer," I say, flashing her a smile.

She scoffs and swats my arm. "No way."

That little move has her wobbling a bit, so I steady her with one hand. I lean in so my words are a whisper in her ear.

"In that case, I promise to uphold your purity." I squeeze her arm slightly, noting the goose bumps rising on her skin.

She leans back a little to meet my eyes. Searching.

"I'm not so pure," she says in a low voice, and fuck if I don't feel all my blood rush from my head into my sorely neglected cock. "I've done things before."

"Makes sense. Men must be lining up," I say, fighting off a smirk.

I'm not sure if it's the alcohol, her proximity, or Oliver's words finally getting through to me, but suddenly, I don't want to hide the attraction I have for her. It's not like she didn't feel it when she was splayed over my lap earlier today, my dick hard against her warm center. And for some reason, when I'm with her, it's easy to forget she works for me.

"So what if they are?" she asks with a playful look, her head tilting.

The dim light of the overhead fixture catches her eyes, and I'm struck speechless for a moment. She's beautiful. Stunning, even.

"What are you waiting for, then?" My mouth is just inches from hers now. There's no more eye contact, just the connection of our mingling breaths.

"Love."

Are you fucking serious?

I pull back. I'm about ready to ravish this woman, and as soon as she brings up the L-word, I'm as soft as a bowl of pudding. Turning away, I pinch the bridge of my nose.

Fuck. I need some space.

"What?" she asks, bewildered by my shift in mood.

"It's a fraud." I turn back with a shrug.

"What is?"

"Love."

"So you've had your heart broken," she says, her voice like a nurse's just before administering a shot.

And yeah, I'll admit, it stings that she's pegged me so quickly.

"More than once," I say, not trying to hide the cynicism in my voice. "I'm not exactly looking for the 'real deal'."

Been there, done that. Women have tried before to save me from myself, from my doubts and self-made walls, to no avail.

"That's why you hire escorts," she says.

Presley has me cornered and she knows it. I'm on her examining table, and she's going to keep poking and prodding until she gets the complete diagnosis.

Not if I have anything to say about it.

"Tell me about your past relationships," she says.

"Pass."

She rolls her eyes. This may be a casual conversation to her, but it's pretty jarring for me. I realize I have my fists clenched at my sides. Fighting for control, I relax my hands.

"You're not married are you?" she asks, voice unsure.

My eyes flash to hers. "God, Presley, of course not. Do you really think what happened in the limo would have if I were married?"

She takes a deep breath, shaking her head. "I didn't think so. But I had to ask." She steps toward me, her eyes like flashlights into my darkest corners. "Okay, let's try an easier question. What's the most romantic thing you've ever done for someone?"

"I'm not really romantic." I rub my thumb across my lip, my eyes never straying from her.

"Come on, there must have been something."

"An all-expenses-paid trip around the world."

Her eyes widen, and her jaw hangs open. "Seriously?"

"And a thousand Persian roses, with little dewdrops made of diamonds. Oh, and one time, horseback riding, but we were both naked—"

She bursts out laughing. "All right, fine. I get it."

I can't help the genuine smile tugging on my lips.

She's still giggling when I slide one arm around her waist to assist with her lack of balance, and help her sit down on the edge of the bed. *Our bed.*

"Whoa, there . . ."

As soon as she's settled, she releases a pleased sigh, her cheeks rosy with laughter. I kneel on the carpet before her, our hands intertwined in her lap.

"You're so graceful," I say, lifting an eyebrow.

She rolls her eyes. "Oh, shut up. I already know I'm not anything like your fancy escorts."

"No, you're not."

Her face galls, but then I lift her hand to my lips, and press a soft kiss there that's reminiscent of our first date. She sucks in a quiet breath, her chest rising with anticipation.

Looking at her now with her long dark hair mussed, her little black dress pushing and pulling at her body in all the right ways . . . I want her. Before I can think too hard about it, I lean into her and inhale against her neck. She shivers.

I could tease this woman forever and never get bored.

Presley isn't in the mood to be teased, however. She yanks at my tie, her lips making contact with my throat as she kisses a little line across my Adam's apple.

I release a sharp exhale and lift her chin, pressing my lips to hers. Presley's hooded eyes sink closed.

My kisses start soft, just chaste presses of my lips to hers. But ever eager to please, Presley parts her lips, and then I'm tasting her. Wine mixes with the sweet flavor of Presley as our tongues touch. She makes a soft, hungry noise in the back of her throat as I thread my hands through her silky hair, tilting her head back.

Pressing hot, hungry kisses against her neck, I'm eager to hear more of the sounds she made in the car. I promised I'd take my time with her, but she's testing my patience like no other woman has.

My lips never leave her skin as I lay her back onto the bed, and we roll into the center together. Her fingers curl into the fabric of my shirt. Her body is so warm, so soft. I want to pin her down, press myself against her, claim her . . .

When she murmurs my name, I drag my teeth lightly across her collarbone, and her hips jolt. My hand slides down her side to cup her round ass, pulling her firmly against me. The way she rubs against me, I can tell that she feels my hard length against her thigh.

"Tell me," I whisper as I kiss down her chest.

I can tell she's aching for me to touch her breasts. I want to, but not as badly as I want her to want it. Massaging her perfect ass with one hand, I trail the other in a tantalizing line down her breastbone. Lower and lower, I drag my fingertips lightly over the soft material of her dress.

"T-tell you what?" She can hardly speak, she's so turned on.

"What sort of things have you done before?" I slide my fingers up the back of her dress, over the skin of one smooth thigh, and reach the dangerously soft skin of her hips and waist. I play with the string of her thong, lifting it from her hip bone and pulling it down, ever so slowly. From my vantage point, I can see her chest rising and falling.

"I don't know . . . Things," she says, then gasps with a swallow.

On my knees now, situated between her legs, I lightly graze my fingers down the center of her belly toward the juncture between her thighs. She sucks in another breath, her hips wiggling on the bed.

Patience, Presley.

"What sort of things?" Giving a tug to the skimpy fabric, I pull her thong down to her ankles. I kiss her knees as I untangle it from her heels, sliding the silken material into my pocket. "Things like this?"

I lick the line of her inner thigh, punctuating the trail with a hard suck. She moans and then laughs a little, breathlessly. I push her dress up on her hips, revealing her perfect pink pussy. *Fucking hell, is there anything more beautiful?*

"Or things like this?" I bring my lips to the needy spot between her thighs, but I don't touch her yet, using my hot breath to drive her crazy.

"Mmm," she whimpers, and my cock presses painfully against my zipper.

Fuck patience.

I part her with my tongue, tasting her with a confident motion. She groans, pushing herself against my mouth. Between soft kisses to her sweet center, I find myself moaning. The vibrations send her reeling, her fingers finding purchase in my hair.

Now that I have her taste on my tongue, I can't stop. I press my tongue into her warmth and almost come in my fucking pants. She's so sweet. So tight and tempting. Her fingers rake against my scalp, and she makes needy noises of pleasure.

I hook my thumbs around her hip bones to give myself more leverage against her eager motions. She's panting with short, high-pitched breaths that tell me she's close to coming. Focusing on her clit, I suck away at her last efforts of composure.

"Dom!" she shouts.

Presley.

I slide one hand up her body to find her breast, pulling a nipple between forefinger and thumb. With the most maddening, soft whimpering sounds I've ever heard, Presley grinds herself right against my face, and I'm lost.

CHAPTER FOURTEEN

Presley

I've never felt anything so intense. My thighs quake and my hips shove against Dominic's mouth in uncontrollable desperation, in my need to be even closer. The sensation is almost too much, but I'm not about to back down now. I'm so close, so maddeningly close.

"Please," I whimper. "I can't take it, don't stop!"

I'm not making any sense, but it doesn't matter when his incredible tongue is flooding me with so much pleasure. He growls into me, and the vibration and the fiery hunger in his eyes when they scan mine tip me over.

Writhing, I stifle a scream as the most powerful orgasm I've ever had crashes through me. It goes on and on, and he doesn't let up until I'm trembling with oversensitivity, and left feeling dazed and limp.

Holy hell!

Dominic smirks from between my legs with wolfish satisfaction. "Good, I take it?"

I nod slowly, still hazy. *Good* doesn't even begin to cover it. I've just had my mind blown—by my boss. *Oh God.*

But I'm not going to question whether this is right or wrong. Not anymore, or at least, not tonight. Right now, I'm just eager to return the favor. The endorphins rushing through my bloodstream have commanded my brain to pipe down, and my body is the one doing the thinking.

The moment he gets back on the bed to kiss me, I'm fumbling for his shirt buttons with shaky fingers. He lets out a pleased hum as I unbuckle his belt. Together, we struggle to strip him and toss his clothes over the side of the bed without breaking our kiss.

With my eyes and hands, I devour each new inch of his exposed skin. His naked body is perfect, every angle and muscle sculpted by a classical artist. And when he slips off his boxers and his hard length springs free, my body gives an involuntary clench.

"You are unfairly hot," I mumble.

He laughs. "Glad you appreciate the view."

It's an amazing one. But after so many days of being forced to content myself with just looking, I'm not waiting another second to taste. I scoot down his body to straddle his lower legs and bring my face close to his cock. Long, thick, flushed, and dripping . . . all because of me. I did this to him.

And now I get to do a lot more. I lick my lips.

He blinks. "You don't have to."

"I know, but I want to." *So damn bad.* I've been repressing fantasies about it since my first day at Aspen.

He strokes my hair. "Are you sure? Don't do anything you're not comfortable wi—"

I shut him up by closing my mouth around him, and I relish how his breath hitches and his hand stills in my hair.

"Shit. If you're sure." He releases a sharp exhale, then a husky noise. He rests one hand on my head and the other on my shoulder. "Go on, baby."

The sweet name is unexpected, and out of place, but I like it much more than I thought I would. Because it came from Dominic, the always in control, always so disciplined man who's walls are tumbling down just for me.

I hesitate, because now I actually have to figure out what I'm doing. Experimentally, I lick a line from base to tip. *Wow, the skin is so soft*. I taste the salt of his sweat and a hint of musk—definitely not unpleasant, especially with the quiet sigh that escapes him.

Holding him firmly by the base, I slide my lips toward my hand. My gag reflex asserts itself long before I hit bottom. Okay, not what I wanted, but I can work with this. Treat it like a popsicle, I guess. I lick and suck my way back up, then down again, and his soft groan of pleasure electrifies me. Encouraged, I continue.

"A little more—*fuck*, just like that. You're doing amazing." He groans, caressing from my shoulder, up my neck, and over my cheek. "God, look at you. Those pretty lips wrapped around me . . . You're so sexy, it should be illegal."

In appreciation of the compliment, I take a little more of him. His fingers knot in my hair, half directing me, half just holding on.

Letting his touch and his sensual noises guide me, I bob my head faster and swirl my tongue as I grow more confident in my technique. I see why people enjoy this—it's so hot to hear him unravel bit by bit, so heady to learn I can make such a powerful man gasp my name, bring him so much pleasure that his muscular stomach and thighs begin to quiver.

His grip tightens spasmodically, sending pain-pleasure sparks from my scalp all the way down my spine. "Presley . . . I'm about to . . ."

I don't stop. I want everything he can give me.

When I suck harder, he groans loud and rough, his thick, hot release pulsing over my tongue. I swallow, shocked at how intensely bitter it tastes, but still craving every drop.

"Damn . . ." He breathes out the word, and a swell of pride fills my chest.

The hand buried in my hair relaxes, caressing instead of clenching. I let my head drop into his warm lap and luxuriate in the way he's softly stroking the long locks of my hair.

Then he adds, "That was pretty good. For an intern."

I grab a pillow and toss it at his face. The cocky jerk just laughs. But it's okay, because I'm giggling, too.

"I think it's time for bed. Or do you not take suggestions from *interns*?" I say, returning the jab with my eyebrows raised in mock rebuke.

We're still naked and this should feel strange, but his playful remark seems to have relaxed the charged atmosphere around us. Who knows, maybe that's why he said it? He seems to know his way around most social situations. Even the awkward moment after you've just had spontaneous oral sex with an employee, I mean, intern.

Oh God, I wonder if he's been in this situation before?

I won't let myself spiral with worry right now. Endorphins are still pulsing through my system, and I'm determined not to worry. At least, not yet. I'm sure there will be time for regrets and examination of my behavior come morning.

Dominic gazes down at me fondly, touching my cheek one last time as he holds my gaze. I see the hint of a smile on his lips, and then he swings his legs over the side of the bed and tugs on his black boxer briefs. "I think I agree. Roger the others were about to call it a night too."

We dig our toiletries out of our suitcases. With two sinks, the bathroom is roomy enough for us to stand side by side while we brush our teeth. Normally, I'd be a little self-conscious, but it feels natural. Comfortable. Almost . . . domestic. I push away the dangerous thought.

After changing into pajamas, I slip beneath the covers, wiggling a little to enjoy their soft, silky slide. Everything feels so good—I'm still languid and sensitive from earlier. Though I'm sure it doesn't hurt that our guest bed comes equipped with linens worthy of a five-star hotel.

Dominic glances up from his suitcase to shoot me a soft smile that I don't dare call *affectionate*. "You look comfortable. Sleep well."

"You're not coming to bed?"

He pulls out his laptop and sets it on the desk. "In a bit. There's a little more work I wanted to get done first."

I'm a little disappointed, but mostly just amused. How typical of a workaholic CEO. "Good night, boss."

He chuckles as he turns off the bedside lamp. "Good night, intern. Let me know if the light bothers you."

Although the night has worn me out, for a little while I let my gaze rest on him, silhouetted by the soft glow of his screen. He really is an amazing man. Hardworking to a fault, sweet when he wants to be, a skilled and generous lover . . . even though he's made it clear that he doesn't believe in love.

My eyes grow heavier. I drift off to the quiet noise of tapping keys.

• • •

I'm woken by Dominic nudging me and saying something.

"Wha . . . ?" I squint up at him in the bright morning sunlight.

"We have to go," he says insistently.

I rub my eyes with one hand and grope for my phone with the other. "What time is it?"

"It's after ten." Before I can ask, he adds, "You slept through breakfast. I had Roger's valet put a few muffins in the limo for you to eat while we drive."

Wow, I almost never sleep this late. I guess he wore me out last night.

I'm about to crack a joke about his prowess when I finally get a good enough look at him to realize something's off. Dominic is unshaven, and his hair is disheveled. His face is tense, his brow furrowed and lips tight.

"What's wrong?" I ask. It must be bad if he's this frazzled.

"There's been an incident. We need to get back to the city ASAP. Hurry and get dressed. I've already said good-bye to Roger for us."

An incident? I have no idea what he means, but

I sense now's not the time to ask any more questions. I roll onto my feet, then get dressed and pack as fast as I can.

Outside on the driveway, the limo is waiting, its engine running. As soon as we're seated and the door is shut, Dominic is on the phone before the chauffeur has even hit the gas.

"How's Emilia?" His tone is low and urgent, his expression grave. If I didn't know better, I'd say there was fear in his eyes.

The voice on the other end sounds like a woman, but I can't quite make out her words.

I try to eat my muffin without getting crumbs all over the upholstery or making it too obvious that I'm straining to eavesdrop. When he said *incident,* I assumed it was of a business nature. This sounds like something much more personal.

"What did the doctor say?" he asks.

He listens for several minutes, during which his expression gradually loosens.

"Thank God." He pulls his hand down over his mouth, suddenly looking much older than his twenty-six years. "So you're still at the hospital?"

The woman says something else.

"Okay. I'll go home, then. But first, can you explain one more thing to me?" A silent pause. "When she fell, just where the hell were you?"

I almost flinch at the steel in his voice. Whoever is on the other end, she's in deep shit.

Several more minutes pass of her talking.

Finally, he sighs. "I guess it couldn't be helped. See you in . . ." He checks his watch. "An hour and forty-five minutes." He hangs up.

I ache to ask him what's going on, but he's staring out the window with a brooding expression, clearly not in the mood to be bothered. Confused, I fold my muffin paper into a smaller and smaller square as I try to piece together what I've overheard.

Who the heck is Emilia? I know from my research that Dominic had a father and an older brother. His mother passed away when he was a toddler, and I've never heard about any other important woman in his life. Emilia's falling made Dominic panic, so unless she plummeted off a building or something, she's probably either very young or very old. A little sister? A grandmother? An elderly aunt?

Whoever she is, the woman on the phone got this Emilia medical attention right away, and it seems like she'll be okay. I'm glad to hear that much. But I still burn with curiosity, and I hope all my questions will be answered when we get to Dominic's place.

CHAPTER FIFTEEN

Dominic

Sunlight flashes brightly through the windows of the limo. I keep my gaze on the passing landmarks and road signs, silently noting how much longer it will take to get home. *My sweet little Emilia.*

Fran called to tell me that the smaller of my twins had fallen and smacked her head on the marble floor in the kitchen. She'd called the pediatrician's office immediately. Apparently, it's nothing major. Doesn't mean I didn't lose my shit at the thought of my two-year-old having a head injury.

The sounds of the road and the glare of the sun don't help this throbbing stress headache in the slightest. I don't realize that my leg is bouncing incessantly until Presley puts a warm hand on my knee. She's been sitting right next to me this whole time, quiet and close.

At her touch, my knee stills, but I can't force myself to look at her. I don't want her to see me like this. I have a hunch that the moment she looks into my eyes, she'll see through everything I've been trying to protect, right past the guarded walls and into my personal life. I'm trying not to panic about that.

Presley is going to have questions. I had to pull her away from our arrangement abruptly, skipping breakfast and good-byes. Dragging her into my personal life was the last thing I wanted to do, at least under these circumstances. I appreciate how understanding she's been, despite the strangeness of the situation, but she doesn't need to be a part of this.

But I realize we're already here, at my apartment.

I open the door before we've entirely come to a stop, ready to make a break for the entrance. Presley is scooting out right behind me. Before her feet touch the ground, I catch her hand.

"Don't worry, the driver can take you home."

"Is everything okay?" she asks in a small voice. The kindness in her eyes tells me she's genuinely worried.

That makes two of us.

"I don't know," I admit. Eager to get inside, I make a snap decision I hope I don't regret later. "Come on."

The car door swings closed behind us, and we move quickly toward the building. I use my keycard to unlock the heavy glass door. I hold it wide for Presley, who then jogs to the first empty elevator and presses the UP button.

She turns to me, her expression serious and calm. "Which floor?"

"Twelve."

The usually charming ding of the elevator passing each floor is infuriating today as it rises excruciatingly slow and the doors take their damn sweet time opening. I jam my thumb onto the button repeatedly, trying to force the elevator to move faster.

Presley's warm fingers find mine. My hand curls around hers, and I don't miss the reassuring squeeze she gives me. When the doors finally open about ten years later, I drag her down the hall, then pull out my keys and unlock the door in one fluid motion.

"Fran?" I call into the empty foyer.

"Daddy!"

The familiar squeals of my girls precede their running feet, and in seconds, I'm on my knees with my arms outstretched. They maul me with their little hands, burying their faces in my shoulders. I examine Emilia's head, finding a large pink lump on her forehead.

"Baby, what happened?"

"Boo-boo." She whimpers with a big frown, her eyes welling up.

I pull her into me, kissing the top of her head. Lacey tangles her fingers in her sister's hair.

"I'm so sorry," I murmur, wiping away the tears that spill from Emilia's bright eyes.

"Don't cry." Lacey hiccups, a sure sign she'll soon be falling to pieces after her sister.

"All right, girls." Fran hobbles around the corner and down the hall. She stops in her tracks when she sees us, tilting her head with an obvious question as she stares at me. *Who is this beautiful young woman you've brought home with you?*

It sure as hell doesn't happen often. I don't think Fran's ever seen me with a woman, come to think of it.

Presley is frozen, her hands grasped in front of her. I almost chuckle when I see her expression—with wide eyes and her mouth hanging open.

"Hello, young lady," Fran says, her voice warm.

"Hello." Presley gives her a cautious smile.

"I'm the nanny, Francine."

"Oh, I'm the—I'm . . ." Presley looks to me as if to say, *What the hell am I to you?*

"She's a coworker." I push to my feet, and the girls wrap themselves around my legs.

"Oh, a coworker." Fran raises her eyebrows to me.

"So nice to meet you," Presley says, one hand outstretched. It's so fucking adorable how polite she is when she's confused.

Fran gives Presley's hand a brisk shake. "Nice to meet you." To me, she says with a wink, "I'll be off, then. Too many cooks in the kitchen." And just like that, Fran has her coat and her mammoth purse in her hands, and she leaves us.

I imagine what the scene must look like from Presley's perspective, her twenty-six-year-old boss with a tiny human clinging to each leg.

"Presley, meet the two women in my life."

"Hi," she says softly, wiggling her fingers at the girls.

Lacey waves back, while Emilia buries her face deeper into my pant leg.

"These are my daughters, Lacey and Emilia."

A small, incredulous smile creeps onto Presley's face. "You're a father?"

• • •

Ten minutes later, I'm at the kitchen counter, slicing grapes in half. The only way I could peel the girls from my legs was to suggest snack time. Of course it had to be their favorite—animal crackers and grapes.

Presley sits across from Lacey and Emilia. She clearly has a mouthful of questions. But instead of asking them, she talks to the girls in hushed tones, telling the story of each animal cracker as it's pulled from the bag.

"Monkey is very good at climbing. He won all the competitions on the playground. Giraffe is a little annoyed about that, since he's as tall as the highest ladder already."

Lacey and Emilia are completely enamored with her, hanging on her every word.

"Ladder?" Emilia asks in a small voice.

"You know like a slide?" Presley asks, and Emilia nods. Presley pantomimes gripping the rungs of a ladder, climbing up. "Ladders help you get up to the slide."

Lacey follows suit, as she always does.

"See, you're a monkey!" Presley says, and Lacey giggles.

I bring two bowls of grapes to the table, handing them each one. My girls reach for them with greedy fingers, and soon juice dribbles down their chins. I use the corner of my sleeve to wipe Lacey's mouth. When I glance over, Presley is staring at me with a look of . . . fascination? Admiration? I'm not sure.

This is way too weird.

"I'm sure you have to get back," I say, trying to regain control of the situation.

"Not really," Presley says with a small shrug.

"It's no trouble. I'll get you a car." I pull out my phone to make the call, but both of my girls erupt into sheer outrage.

"No! Presley, stay!" they cry, their eyes wide and pleading.

Fuck. Now I'm going to have to deal with this all night.

"Presley has work to do," I say, unsure if that is even true.

Presley frowns, but takes the cue and stands from the table. *Good girl.*

"I'll see you again, monkeys," she says, tucking a stray hair behind Emilia's ear and winking at

Lacey. "Okay?"

"Okay," they mumble, scowling.

After I've arranged the pickup, I escort Presley to the front door. When we reach the door, she turns to me. I can see the anxious and sensitive questions on the tip of her tongue.

You're a father?

Why do you keep it a secret?

Where is their mother?

Anything she says will make my heart wrench uncomfortably, and I don't want to feel that shit right now. So before the words escape her lips, I kiss her. Hard.

Backing her against the wall, I let my mouth steal away anything she might have said that would make me feel anything. I lick her tongue and feel her shudder against me, her fingers grasping my shirt. Her hand slides up my chest to rest against my cheek in a gesture so tender, my heart clenches painfully.

I release her, and when I pull back, her eyes are glazed with emotion. With expectation.

I never should have brought her here.

Fighting for control, I straighten my shoulders. I open the door and avert my gaze. Presley is an open book that I don't want to read at this moment. "Thanks for your work this weekend. Extra points for giving good head."

She pulls in a sharp intake of breath at my crudeness. Even from my peripheral vision, I can see her stunned expression.

I straighten my posture and hold open the door wider. "Look, last night was fun, but it can't happen again. There are rules for a reason and we will not be crossing them. Come Monday morning, I'm your boss and you are one of the many interns trying for a position with Aspen Hotels." The words leave me in a rush, but I'm thankful that I sound more composed than I feel. I'm fucking rattled. And I hate being rattled.

Presley lifts her chin and gazes out the door, and without saying anything else, she leaves.

CHAPTER SIXTEEN

Presley

On Monday morning, I station myself at my desk, hoping that throwing myself into work will distract me.

I was up half the night with my thoughts running wild. The topic? None other than my sexy-assin and equally infuriating boss. Which is so not helpful to my sanity.

I walked into our deal knowing it was all for the sake of wooing a client, yet I thought we'd made a real connection, deeper than just boss and intern. The laughter. The flirting. The kissing. But it turns out our fake relationship really is nothing but fake. How could I be so naïve?

My eyes burn for reasons that have nothing to do with sleep deprivation, and my computer screen blurs. I blink fast to chase away impending tears.

Get a grip, Pres.

Yes, I misjudged everything and it feels awful, but am I going to collapse or stand back up on my own two feet? I need to let go and fix my mistakes like a big girl. And that starts with cutting my losses, right this minute.

From now on, I'll refuse to see that prick except during business hours at the office. The next time he comes waltzing up to ask for a date, I'm telling him our deal is off. No more "overtime" for me. Let him figure out on his own how to lie to Roger about where I am. I've made some of the money I needed toward Michael's bills, and I care about myself to much to get emotionally involved with such a total asshole.

Well, to be fair, he's not one hundred percent an asshole. Yesterday afternoon, he seemed like a great dad. The way he fussed over his daughters was pretty damn adorable. Watching his strong forearms as he lifted them. Fussing over their snack and slicing those grapes in half. It was downright disarming to see such a different side of him . . .

I slam the brakes on that train of thought. *Dam-*

mit, stop mooning over him like a schoolgirl. He's already hurt me once—what more will it take to get it through my head that he's a jerk? The way he thanked me for that blow job made me feel about ten inches tall. Like he was buying a pack of gum or something. Who talks about sex like that, as if it was just a transaction?

But sex is a transaction to him, a nasty little voice whispers in my head. Did you forget that he only screws women he's paid for? *He told you that himself. You were just too blinded by infatuation to really believe it.*

My hands slow on the keyboard. Is that . . . how he feels about me? Does he see what we shared on Saturday night as something he purchased?

I shake my head. No more dwelling on it. I'm here to work, and I need to pull my focus back to that. I just have to accept that we come from worlds too different to be compatible, and move on . . . no matter how right it felt to be in his arms.

A knock on my cubicle wall mercifully interrupts my sour thoughts. I spin my chair around, expecting Jordan, only to see Aspen's vice president.

"G-good morning, Mister—"

"I told you, there's no need to be so formal. Please call me Oliver." He flashes me a reassuring smile. "And relax, I came with good news. I just wanted to stop by and let you know what a great job you did on that budget proposal."

I blink, flustered that a VP would come praise me in person. "Oh, thank you. Jordan helped a lot, too."

I regret the words as soon as they're out of my mouth. It's true that he worked hard on this assignment, but I can't afford to undercut my achievements with good-girl modesty.

"Sure, it was a partnered project, but the quality of your contribution was clear. You really went above and beyond."

I can't hold back a grin. "Thank you so much. That really means a lot to me."

"It's the truth. Keep up the good work, okay, Presley?" Oliver shoots a pair of finger guns at me and strolls off.

I will. From now on, I'm all business. I'm going to put my nose to the grindstone, prove that I'm the best intern here, and snag that job. I'll rise above all the ridiculous crap that's happened and take my power back from Dominic, no matter if he is our industry's cocky young darling.

My phone dings. I check it and almost laugh at the perfect timing. It's a text from Austin, asking if I can see him again tonight. What better way to try to forget Dominic and his "dates" than to go on an actual date with an actual nice guy? What a concept.

I fire off a quick text to tell him I'm in, and then get back to my daily hustle.

• • •

My buzz of renewed purpose lasts all day. But it wavers when I walk into the bar's lounge and see Austin sitting with his brow knitted in a grave frown, jiggling his leg and chewing his lip.

The instant he spots me, he jumps up. "Presley! It's great to see you."

I hug him cautiously. "You, too. Is everything all right?"

"Not . . . really. Go ahead and sit down. I'll get

us drinks first before I explain." When he returns from the bar with two beers, he asks, "Are you familiar with Genesis Software?"

"I know the name," I reply slowly. "All I know about them is what I heard on the news last year. They caused that big data breach—"

"More like we were blamed for it."

The edge in Austin's tone surprises me, coming from a guy who's usually so laid-back and friendly. Then I realize what he just let slip.

"Wait, *we*? You work for Genesis?"

"My father owns it. And when Aspen Hotels bad-mouthed us to the press, he lost almost everything. Our stock price nose-dived, and we had to lay off six-thousand employees."

My stomach sinks, and my brain struggles to catch up with his accusation. "You blame Aspen for this?"

"Your CEO—Dominic, was it? His official stance was that the breach at Aspen was our fault, and since the moment he said that, everything's been crumbling."

This is headed nowhere good. I work for Aspen, and that's where my allegiance lies. I'm hoping to win a spot on the management team. Which means I shouldn't be here.

I push out my chair. "I should probably go."

Austin's eyes widen to puppy-dog proportions. "Wait! Please don't go. I have a request, a simple one. Just hear me out."

I'm on my feet; I should already be walking away.

But despite myself, I ask, "What could you possibly want from me? I'm sorry to hear your business is going under, I really am, but I have nothing to do with this. I haven't even been working there for a full month yet."

"I know. I just . . . God, it sounds petty when I say it out loud, but I need you to insert this into his laptop." Before I can back away, he presses a jump drive into my hand.

"What is this?"

"A small virus," he says, as if it's something completely innocuous.

I narrow my eyes. "If it's so small, why do you want me to release it so badly? What will it do?"

"It'll prove to him that he's not the god he thinks he is. He's not immune; his systems can become corrupt, too, and our software isn't the bullshit he claimed it was."

"And why on earth would I jeopardize the company where I'm trying to start my career?"

"Don't worry, you'll still have a job. This won't destroy Aspen, just scare Dominic a little. And I'll pay you enough to make it worth your risk. Didn't you mention you had high expenses?"

"There's no amount of money that could—"

"Please, Presley. I need you to take this for me. It's the right thing to do."

I dodge his attempt to rest a hand on my arm. "I'm sorry, but no way."

"At least think it over. Read this dossier . . ." He sets down a paper-stuffed folder marked with the Genesis logo. "Decide for yourself if we really are the villains he painted us to be."

I don't need to think it over. But before I can

toss his crap back at him, Austin is already gone, leaving me alone with the folder on the table and the jump drive burning in my hand.

I should just throw them both in the trash. No way in hell would I ever infect Dominic's computer. He might be a douchebag when it comes to women, but he's still a skilled CEO, and more importantly, Aspen Hotels doesn't deserve to go down. At least I don't think they do...

At the same time, though, it sounds like there's a lot more to the Genesis story than I was led to believe. Austin has managed to pique my curiosity.

After a minute of hesitation, I stuff it all into my bag to take home. As soon as I get an uninterrupted evening of spare time, I'll read his intel and then dispose of it. At the very least, I can find out the truth.

CHAPTER SEVENTEEN

Dominic

Presley is avoiding me. Again. We're back to square one. She's made it a point to take any path in the office that doesn't cross my door. I haven't seen her for longer than three seconds at a time all week long. She's just working hard, I keep telling myself.

"Extra points for giving good head."

What the fuck was that? I completely reverted to the frat boy I never intended to be. Speaking of which—

"Got a sec?" Oliver asks, poking his head through my doorway.

I've been staring at my in-box, unable to focus on any one task long enough to do work. A second won't hurt. I wave him in.

As always, Oliver makes himself at home right away. In less than a minute, the door is closed and ice is clinking at the bottom of a fresh glass of scotch. With a heaving sigh, Oliver sinks into the wingback chair across from my desk.

Suddenly, I'm hit with the sensation of déjà vu. We were in this exact same place only two weeks ago. I chuckle.

"What?" he asks, his eyebrows furrowed.

"Nothing." I sigh. *What a simpler time.*

Oliver stares at me over the rim of his tumbler. "Hmm."

"What?" It's my turn to ask.

"What'd you do to piss off your intern?"

"What are you talking about?"

"Did you two fuck?"

"No." I'm not sure Oliver entirely believes me, and he shakes his head in dismay. "But I told her," I add.

"Told her what?"

"About my girls."

At first, Oliver looks confused. Then shocked. Then intrigued. "Damn."

Tell me about it. "What do you think about that?" I want to know if he thinks I made a mistake. Hell, I want to know if *I* think if I've made a mistake. There's a reason I haven't gone public about my daughters. I don't want the media's attention.

"I think that's a big deal."

"I know." I lean forward, holding my head in my hands. A tension headache is starting to form and my neck feels stiff.

Oliver's hand on my shoulder brings me back. "Let's take off early."

I open my mouth to object, but he swipes my car keys off my desk too fast. Unable to help it, I crack a smile.

I don't deserve his friendship, but I damn sure need it.

• • •

"Guess who's here?"

My girls stare up at me with big eyes, practically bouncing with excitement. Just behind me in the hallway waits Uncle Oliver, their favorite surprise guest.

"Who? Who?"

Fran shakes her head and chuckles at their excitement. "Not that young woman, I suppose," she says with a wry smile.

I give her a look to say *don't get their hopes up.*

"Say good night to Franny first. Then I'll tell you."

"'Night!" they cry, impatient.

The sweet woman kisses them each on the cheek—and one extra on Emilia's bruise.

When Oliver steps inside, the girls squeal with excitement.

"Uncle Oliver! Up! Up!" Lacey cries.

He lifts her like she's a bag of flour and places her on his shoulders. Emilia takes his hand, her tiny one completely engulfed in his much larger one.

"Look," she says, pointing to her forehead.

"Oh my! What's that?"

"A bruise."

"From what?"

"I fell."

"Oh no." Oliver kneels down, Lacey still perched on his shoulders. "You know, I get bruises, too."

"Why?"

"Well, when Auntie Jess gets angry with me—"

"Okay," I say quickly, pulling Emilia up onto my shoulders.

I shoot him a look, and he smirks at me. What a fucking goof.

Tonight, there are no rules. We eat our roasted veggie dinner picnic-style on the kitchen floor with Uncle Oliver, who barely gives the girls a chance to eat their carrots between tickles.

"Promise me you will never, never, never-ever like a boy," Oliver says, pinky finger outstretched. They both reach out and hold his finger with their tiny hands.

"You're a boy," Emilia says, ever the rational one.

"Only me, then."

"And Daddy," Lacey says, reaching for my hand.

I set down my fork and kiss her little fingers before pretending to gobble them up. "Cheers to that," I say, lifting my beer to Oliver's.

"Cheers!" he says. "Lift your cup!"

The girls lift their sippy cups and giggle. Oliver is a hit with kids, always has been, always will be.

I find myself wondering what life would be like if . . . well, if I were Uncle Dominic instead of Daddy. Coming into someone else's home, simply to wreak controlled havoc until bedtime, and then going back to my own bachelor life. Choices unhindered by—

No.

That's not what I want. These girls are my life now. I wouldn't have it any other way.

For some reason, the image of Presley comes to mind. I remember exactly how she looked, sitting across from my daughters at the kitchen table. Her smile was warm and her eyes full of wonder as she whispered with them. Her soft hair fell in messy waves across her shoulders. She was disheveled from the abrupt departure that morning, but she didn't mind at all. She was there, in the moment, giving Emilia and Lacey her undivided attention.

And then I went and ruined it.

Like a total asshole.

I stand up from the kitchen floor with a stretch, dishes in hand. Oliver has the girls hanging on his every word, particularly the part where he agrees to come to their tea party, which is scheduled for right now. It's easy for me to pull out my cell phone and send a quick text. Which is probably a bad idea, but that doesn't stop me.

```
I can't stop thinking about
you.
```

Yes. Definitely a bad idea. Minutes pass before my phone buzzes.

Me or my mouth?

I surprise myself by laughing. *Shit.* I deserve that.

You.

No response.

I said some stupid shit. I do that when I'm scared.

What am I even saying? How do I articulate this? How do I—

I scare you?

Can I call?

Sure.

Let me put the girls down first.

Okay.

With the dishes in the sink, I turn back to the tea party on the floor. "All right, girls, what time is it?"

"No!" Lacey whines, knowing exactly what time it is.

"Bath time." Emilia stands and dutifully plants the most charming little kiss on Oliver's cheek.

"Wow, thank you so much," he says with a chuckle. "I'll see you guys soon, okay? We'll continue this tea party. Half the guests haven't even arrived yet."

"Okay." Lacey pouts, clearly unsatisfied with this, but being such a good girl.

The three of us all see Uncle Oliver to the door. When he's gone, I take the girls to the tub in the master bath for one of their favorite rituals—bath time. There's minimal splashing tonight; Oliver has them good and tuckered out. When footie-pajamas are on and the girls are snug in their beds, I only have to read a few pages of *Goodnight Moon* for them to sail away into their dreams.

I owe you one, Oliver.

I sneak away to my bedroom, cell phone in hand. I've been anxious to call Presley and explain myself, but it occurs to me I don't know what I'll even say. I sit on the edge of my bed, staring at our texts.

Fuck it.

The phone rings three times before she answers.

"Hello?" Her voice is as smooth as that first sip of ice-cold whiskey.

I swallow. "Hey."

"Hi," she says cautiously.

"What are you up to?" Small talk couldn't hurt. Maybe I'll find my bearings somewhere in conversation.

"Oh, just cards."

"Tarot?" I am so fascinated by this hobby of hers.

"Yeah."

"What does it say?" Hopefully nothing about leaving insensitive assholes in the past.

"I don't know yet."

I can hear her smile through the phone. Good. She can still smile when speaking to me. Maybe all hope isn't lost.

"Did I interrupt?"

"It's okay. There's no time limit."

"So I can talk to you all night, that's what you're saying?"

She laughs. The sound floods my head, eradicating any remnants of the tension that has been gripping my temples for days.

"Well, that depends," she says, tone careful.

"On what?"

"Rumor has it there's an apology coming."

I grin at her boldness. Presley is certainly unlike any other young woman I've met. She catches mc off guard and challenges me. She doesn't care that I'm a powerful, wealthy CEO and that she's just an intern. She pushes my boundaries every single chance she gets. It's refreshing.

"There is. You're right. Again. I'm sorry. I acted

like a dick. I shouldn't have left things like that." The words are true, spoken with the confidence of someone who knows they've royally fucked up and deserve whatever is coming. "I hope you can forgive me."

The line is quiet for a moment. I close my eyes, imagining what her expression might be. I wonder if she's frowning, if there's a crease in her forehead as she weighs my words.

"Apology accepted."

I smile. "Thank you. Can I take you out to dinner?"

"Um," she stammers. "For what? Roger again?"

"No, just dinner."

"Just dinner?"

I can practically see her narrowing her eyes in disbelief. I'd be bracing myself for rejection if I weren't so charmed by her.

"Just dinner. Just us," I say.

She's quiet. I wonder if she's looking at the cards.

"I could do dinner."

And with those words, the universe is on my side for the first time in a long time.

"Tomorrow night, after work," I tell her.

"It's a date," Presley whispers.

CHAPTER EIGHTEEN

Presley

" I think I needed this." Dominic digs a spoon into the oval-shaped dish of lavender crème brûlée.

"The dessert? It *is* pretty amazing," I reply with a grin before I spoon another bite into my mouth.

Looking dead serious, he says, "No, a night off with you."

A wash of giddy delight hits me. The hyper-disciplined CEO who always plays his cards close to the vest not only likes me, but is being open about it. Though he does also tend to be bold and blunt, so maybe I shouldn't be so surprised.

Still, the admission catches me off guard, leaving me feeling almost shy. On cloud nine, mind you, but a little shy all the same. This man is so far out of my league and sexy as all get-out. It's a little disorienting. I shouldn't feel so weak. I shouldn't ache for his hard-won crooked smiles, but I do.

Tonight we've feasted on roasted fish, had one too many glasses of an amazing French wine, and enjoyed casual conversation and laughter. And the best part has been knowing that we aren't putting on a show for anyone. Now I know for sure that Dominic really does care about me, and he isn't just pretending for the sake of keeping up appearances with Roger or getting into my pants. Although I definitely do want him in my pants, too.

Grinning, I reply, "Tonight's been really fun." I haven't realized until now just how much I missed talking with Dominic so casually. "It means a lot to hear you missed me, too."

"I won't fuck this up again," he says solemnly. He takes my hand, rubbing his thumb across my knuckles, and although the touch is affectionate rather than sexual, it still makes my stomach do a little flip. Then he adds, "Not to say the dessert isn't delicious."

"Mmm . . . I agree." I scrape up the last decadent bite and heave a sigh of mixed delight and disappointment that it's all gone. "That might have been the best thing I've ever tasted."

"But I'm still hungry." Suddenly Dominic's gaze turns smoldering—and I'm caught right in the middle of its fire. "I want to take you home," he whispers, his voice dark.

I shiver with eagerness. "God, I want that, too. So bad."

"But . . ." His wolfish expression sobers for a moment. "We should make sure we're on the same page first."

"About what?"

"About what this is, Presley. Everything I said before still applies. I don't have time for relationships, or have the skill set to see one through, to be honest. No matter how amazing a woman you are, I'm not looking for anything serious. But I like this thing between us. Think you can stay casual?"

I watch him in silent fascination, still trying to make sense of this complicated man seated before me. The man who runs a billion-dollar empire, who's single-handedly raising two sweet toddlers, and who likes to pay for sex . . .

Then the corner of his mouth quirks. "Oh God, you already have a tattoo of my name on your ass, don't you?"

I scoff, then shake my head. "No tattoos. I promise."

"Then what do you say?"

I consider his invitation for a minute. I've never done anything like this before—not only sex, but anything reckless and "just for fun."

What would it be like to throw caution to the wind and take something I want just because I want it? To take a vacation from my good-girl persona?

I always do this, don't I? I always overanalyze every decision.

But I already know what I want. Every cell in my body strains toward Dominic, the heat of my desire pooling low in my belly. So why am I questioning it?

For once in my life, I want to try doing something different. *Be* someone different.

I've never been this confused. This lost. It's

disorienting but I'd be lying if I said I didn't love it.

Dominic's fingers trace lightly over my wrist where my pulse thrums out an unsteady rhythm.

"I think I'm okay with staying casual," I say. And it's the truth. I *think* I might be. At least for a little while. Why not see where this goes?

Dominic's eyes spark with desire. He nods at a waiter and says, "Check, please."

• • •

He leads me quickly and quietly into his luxurious apartment and through the darkened halls, straight to his bedroom. "Wait here," he whispers with a soft kiss pressed against my lips.

I hear voices and assume he's letting Francine go for the evening. I set my bag down and take a deep breath.

Moments later, Dominic is back, and there's a hungry, almost predatory look in his eyes. He closes the door and locks it before he turns on a small bed-side lamp, giving the room a soft, romantic glow. Then without warning, he yanks me flush against him, his hungry mouth finding mine. His kiss is exactly as I thought it'd be, consuming and urgent and a little desperate. It mimics my exact emotions in this moment. His bulge presses into my hip like a steel bar, and my body aches in response.

We fall into bed, devouring each other's mouths. Our hands are everywhere—clutching, caressing, tearing at clothes. I can't get his pants off fast enough. My dress falls to the floor, leaving me bare.

With a husky growl of pleasure, he guides me to lie back on the bed so I'm displayed before him, ready for the taking. Suddenly, I realize that *holy shit, this is actually happening*. Dominic Aspen, my boss, the man who's been driving me crazy for what feels like forever, is lying naked on top of me.

He's going to fuck me. I'm about to lose my virginity.

Horny excitement flares in my stomach, and nervousness jitters along with it. My brain gropes for something clever to say but comes up empty.

I blurt, "H-hey there, big guy . . . that's quite an erection," and instantly regret it. What the heck is wrong with me?

But he doesn't laugh at me or stare like I have two heads. He just purrs, "It's all for you. Like it?"

I giggle, feeling a little less tense. "Way too much." Enough that I lose my mind and start talking nonsense, evidently. "Who knew?"

His lips brush my ear, and his hot chuckle sends goose bumps down my neck. "Me."

"Come on, you couldn't have known all along." Or was I really that obvious about it? Did I spend every day at work with a neon sign fuck me, dominic blinking on my forehead?

"I took a highly educated guess."

Smug bastard. Then something else about work occurs to me. "Uh, I should've brought this up before, but what's the company policy on fraternization?"

He blinks down at me, then bursts out laughing. "We're naked in bed together, and you want to discuss that *now*?"

I laugh, too, at the ridiculous picture I must make and my own straitlaced habits. "I know, I know . . ."

"Don't worry about it. I might be your lover here, but at the office, I'm your boss. I can compartmentalize." He kisses me. "I value you for your work, and nothing that happens here will affect that."

Then he's sucking and licking my nipple, his fingers lightly touching between my legs, and I can't think anymore, I can only whine and squirm for him. But I can't make him go faster—he just keeps teasing me at his own pace. Every time I lift my hips into his touch, he merely watches me in curious fascination.

I let out an impatient huff. "H-how long are . . . you gonna keep . . ."

With an infuriating amount of calm, he replies, "I have to make sure you're ready."

I gasp. "I am. So ready."

He grins down at me. "Hmm. That's for me to decide."

One thick finger slides into me, making me moan with pleasure. Then his thumb runs over my slick, swollen flesh, and I can't help rocking my hips against his hand. The motion is slow and teasing.

As he keeps stroking, he eases another finger inside. "Still okay?"

With this one, I can feel myself stretch, but there's no pain, only the hunger for more. "Yes, yes, just please—"

"Be patient, baby."

A third finger enters me. Now it's really a tight fit; there's a tiny zing of pain along with the satisfying fullness. Even so, I rock into his fingers, eager to get to the main event.

The fingers slide out, and I stifle a disappointed noise.

He grabs a condom from his nightstand and rolls it onto his straining shaft. Then he ever so carefully fills me, his cock wonderfully bigger and hotter than his fingers as he slowly pushes inside.

A moan of relief escapes me, and I lift my hips up to meet him. It hurts a little, but so much stronger is the pleasure of finally, *finally* having Dominic inside me. It's different than I imagined it would be. Better in every way possible.

Dominic gazes down at me with heavy-lidded eyes that are filled with his desire for me, and he makes a low sound that rumbles in his chest. He wraps my legs around his lower back and leans forward to kiss me, pushing himself even deeper, wringing a mewl from my throat.

I've never felt so blissfully full. And the pleasure intensifies a thousandfold when he withdraws slightly, then pushes back in. He sets a steady rhythm, each thrust stealing my breath.

"Y-you can go harder." My voice comes out sounding strange, both dazed and hungry.

"I know I can." His voice is a rough, hot rush in my ear. "If you want something, you have to ask for it, intern."

Never one to back down, I tighten my calves around him. "Fuck me harder, then. Show me how you like it."

With an exhale, he pumps his hips faster and I cry out, clawing at his shoulders, my legs struggling to clamp him closer.

Holy shit, *this* is sex? This series of mind-blowing explosions radiating from my core is what

I've been missing out on for all these years? It's better than I could have ever imagined. It's hot and intense, and wet, and my brain scrambles in sixteen different directions.

"You feel incredible," Dominic whispers, his voice coming out deeper. His possessive, burning gaze as he moves above me is almost as overwhelming as the sensation. "It's so good to finally bury my cock inside you. I can't lie—I've wanted you this whole time."

"Me . . . too . . ."

Suddenly, I realize I'm going to come. I open my mouth to tell him, to say something, because don't people do that? But it's too late. I'm already whimpering and quaking, my body clenching around him in wave after wave of pulsing ecstasy.

When I open my eyes, still trying to catch my breath, he's staring down at me like he's very pleased about something.

"That was one of the hottest things I've ever seen." His teeth touch his lower lip. "Fuck, I want you so bad."

"Then take me," I say, panting.

He kisses me hard, groaning into my mouth, and *oh God*, I can feel his length throbbing inside me as he follows me over the edge.

For a minute, we just lie there in a tangled, damp heap. I don't know about him, but I'm exhausted and still drunk on sex.

Brushing a gentle kiss over my lips, he murmurs, "We should probably get cleaned up."

I don't want to leave this afterglow, but I'm sure he's right. After a quick visit to the bathroom, I'm back in his arms, curled up with my head on his chest, sated and so very happy.

It hits me then that I'm not a virgin anymore, but I don't feel the least bit conflicted about it. No uncertainty, no confusion, no need or even urge to consult the cards. For once, my inner self rings through with crystal clarity. This feels right. Here in Dominic's bed is exactly where I want to be.

We lie together in comfortable silence for a little while before Dominic finally lifts his head off the pillow to glance at the clock.

"I'm going to go check on the girls. You need anything?"

I yawn once and press my nose into his neck, enjoying the feel of his stubble against my cheek. "A glass of water, please."

"Of course." He presses a soft kiss to my temple. "Coming right up."

I watch as my sexy-as-sin and just as complicated boss rises to his feet and tugs on a pair of sweatpants. Of course his sweatpants appear to be made of cashmere, which makes me smile. As if I could forget for one single second how sophisticated and wealthy he is.

He gazes down on me fondly once more before strolling from the room to check on his sleeping daughters.

CHAPTER NINETEEN

Dominic

The smooth curve of Presley's back rises and falls with her soft breathing. I'm not quite sure when she fell asleep because I was too busy watching the way the moonlight reflected off her creamy skin, reveling in the pleasurable calm thrumming through me.

What's going to happen, Dom? Are you really going to let her stay the night?

That can't happen. I don't want to have to explain her presence to Fran in the morning, or deal with the possibility of waking up one of the girls while sneaking Presley out. Trying to put a toddler back to sleep at this time of night isn't my idea of postcoital fun.

Presley shifts under my sheet, her thick hair

splayed across my pillows. She nuzzles into the silken material. It occurs to me that she probably can't afford the frivolous things I take for granted, like eight-hundred-thread-count Egyptian cotton sheets.

I don't want to wake her, I decide. Let her sleep for a little while more.

I roll out of bed and slip on the same pair of cashmere pants from earlier. As I tighten the drawstring, I imagine Presley pulling it loose later. The way her eyes look when she . . .

Get it together, man.

I make myself comfortable in the chair adjacent to the bed. I open my laptop, the soft glow of the screen the only light, except for the moon.

Presley's messenger bag lies beside my chair, near my feet. Her laptop is in that bag, the sign of an employee who's willing to drop everything at a moment's notice to get the work done.

She's so damn dedicated, with a work ethic that rivals my own. And it looks like she has plenty of work to do. There's a folder poking out of her bag, likely jostled loose in our eagerness to get to the fucking part of the evening.

I stare at it, wondering. I haven't given her an assignment lately. On one edge of the folder is scrawled a name.

Genesis . . . the software company that tried to ruin me.

I reach over, pick up the folder, and open it. My stomach twists at what I see.

"What are you doing?" Presley sits up in bed, the sheets pooling around her waist, her breasts naked in the dim light of the room. Her eyes are heavy with sleep and her cheeks rosy with warmth.

Meanwhile, I feel like I just swallowed a piece of coal. "What is this?"

Presley squints at the folder as if she's trying to remember. Recognition flits over her features, then fear. "That's not what you think."

"What do I think?"

"It's not my folder."

"Then why do you have it?"

She sits up straighter, her eyes alert now. "A

guy gave it to me."

"A guy." My heart rate is thrumming fast now, and anger boils through my veins.

"Someone I met," she says. "I've only seen him like, three times."

"Are you fucking him, too?" Presley finches at my words, but the adrenaline surging through my veins is too much to ignore. "Is this what you do? Sleep with whomever you think will help with your career?" I keep my tone calm and cold, and she watches me with huge, worried eyes.

I've been in this position before. Usually, though, I don't catch the lie while the bed's still warm. But Presley is young, and obviously sloppy at the ploy. Many women have wanted to bed me for different reasons, although money is usually at the top of that list.

Corporate sabotage is new. And from Presley, of all people? *Fuck.*

My heart jerks painfully inside my chest. I let her into my world. Hell, I didn't just *let* her in, I was the one who invited her, who insisted. She's met my daughters. Fallen asleep in my bed.

Nausea surges up my throat. All the cyber security bullshit we dealt with last year aged me a decade and cost me millions. I can't go through that again.

"I wasn't going to help him." She leans forward in the bed, grasping the sheets in front of her.

That face could be earnest and honest—or it could be a mask. Presley has surprised me more than once with her ability to adapt her personality, depending on who she's with. Why did I think it would be different with me?

"Please, Dom. You have to believe me."

I want to.

I really do.

I pick up my pants from the floor and retrieve my wallet. My chest tight, I pull out its entire contents—likely around twelve hundred dollars. Holding the bills between two fingers, I offer the cash to Presley, inches from her face.

"Here."

"What's this?"

"For tonight's fuck." My tone is cold, completely lacking any empathy.

Confusion and then hurt flash through those crystal-blue eyes as I toss the pile of money onto the bed. "Dom—Dom." Presley jumps to her feet, tearing her clothes over her limbs in a scramble to get dressed.

I turn toward the door so I don't have to see the pain in her eyes. "It's just like you've heard, right? The rumors about me . . . that I can't get off unless money changes hands. There you go. Take your money."

"Dom, please. I'm not lying. I never meant to hurt you. Dominic, please—you have to believe me!"

She's still trying to explain herself when I open the door to the hallway.

"You have to listen to me!"

I turn and look her straight in the eye, my tone calm, almost calculatingly so. "You'll wake up the girls."

Presley's eyes well with tears, and she nods—a tight, business-like nod. This conversation is over. This meeting is adjourned. She turns back into the room, quietly picks up her things, including the cash, I note, and follows me out.

We don't make a sound, our feet silent on the hardwood floors. When we cross into the hall leading to the front door, Presley takes my hand, forcing me to look at her. Her eyes are wild with emotion, but her jaw is set.

"You have to believe me."

"I don't have to do anything. But I recommend that you get off my property before I call the police and have you removed."

"Dom . . ." Her eyes are bright, alert, and locked on mine.

My heart clenches painfully again. "I've paid you for your time. Now go."

The front door clicks behind Presley, and suddenly I'm alone.

Which is exactly the way it should be.

CHAPTER TWENTY

Presley

I spend the rest of the evening tossing and turn-ing on Bianca's couch, searing pain throbbing through my chest whenever I picture the betrayal that was slashed across Dominic's chiseled fea-tures.

I just don't understand how everything fell apart so fast. A few hours ago, I was on a date with Dominic—a real date. I lost my virginity. I was falling hard and fast for the most difficult, most handsome, most brilliant man I'd ever met, and now . . . Now I've not only been dumped, I don't even know if I still have a job to go to on Monday.

The pain in my chest throbs again. My future was looking so promising, and then it all went up in smoke. I choke back another sob. *What the hell am I going to do?*

Besides, there's the not-so-little fact that I still need money, regardless of what happens with my internship. My chest is so tight, I feel like it could shatter into a million pieces at any moment.

I'm just thankful Bianca's not home to witness my pity party. She's out on a date and told me not to expect her tonight, which is for the best. I don't think she'd be too supportive knowing I slept with my boss, and she'd probably want to hunt Austin down and strangle him for what he did. Although, right now, that's an idea I could get behind.

I can't believe I trusted Austin—I thought he was actually into me. I thought he wanted to get to know me as a person, and the entire time he was using me for my connection to Dominic. I'm not normally so gullible. I feel like a complete and total failure. On every level.

I take a deep, shuddering breath and decide the only thing that's going to make me feel any better is talking to my brother. I dial his number, and he picks up on the first ring.

"Hey, sis." His voice comes out strained, in a hurried whisper.

"Hi. Is . . . this a bad time?"

"I'm just at a party with some people from class. Everything okay?"

"Of course," I lie. "Just wanted to talk to you, but it's no problem." My throat is tight and I can hardly get the words out.

"I'll call you tomorrow," he says over the rush of voices in the background. "The payment for my second term is due in ten days. Wanted to make sure you knew."

My stomach drops. "I'll have the money."

"'Kay. Gotta go. Love you."

With that, Michael ends the call, and I'm left alone once again, feeling even worse than before, if that's even possible.

The only silver lining to all of this is that it's the weekend, and I have the next two days to figure out my next move. The thought of not heading into Aspen on Monday morning makes me physically ill. It's just not like me to jeopardize my entire career for a fling with a brooding, older man. I have no idea what got into me.

Actually, I do. Dominic Aspen is a very hard man to ignore. The things he made me feel . . . the way he lit up my entire body, challenged me, mentored me . . . He never treated me like an intern, and I guess that was the thing I liked best.

Then again, maybe he was only doing what he did best—winning me over simply because it served his purposes. Paying me for my time because he knew I wouldn't refuse. Just like he paid for all his other dates.

And with that, an idea pops into my head.

Dominic once mentioned the escort agency he uses for dates. What was its name—Ambrosia? No, it was called Allure. He made escorting sound pretty safe and lucrative. And I already have a little experience with being paid for my companionship . . . so there's that.

Before I can talk myself out of it, I open my laptop to research Allure. Their website is professional and very tasteful—no nudity, although there are pictures galore of staggeringly gorgeous, lingerie-clad women in come-hither poses. It eases my paranoia only slightly. But if Allure was breaking the law, they wouldn't be able to have such an easy-to-find website without the police descending on them, right?

Still, my gut twists with anxiety. The idea of being alone with a male stranger who's paid for my time, who probably has unspoken expectations, who maybe even lied to the agency about what he wanted . . . would I be able to back out? And even if there was no immediate danger, what if anyone found out about this little venture? How safe would my secret be? How would it affect my ability to find another job and get my career back on track?

Terrible what-ifs run rampant through my mind. Yet I also can't forget that there's only a couple of short months until Michael's next semester begins, and he'll need even more money.

I pick up my tarot deck, hesitate, then put it back down. I'm desperate for some hint to help get me out of this mess. But I know that consulting the cards will only illuminate my own intuition . . . and deep down, I already get the feeling that Allure isn't the right path for me.

What else can I do, though? I ruined everything, destroyed Dominic's trust in me, and I'm almost certainly unemployed now. I need to be able to keep feeding myself and putting Michael through school. I need a way to make money until I can find another job, and this is the easiest option I've come up with so far. Or, at least, the quickest.

Maybe it's not as bad as I'm imagining. Maybe I can get a gig where all I have to do is be arm candy, like I did with Dominic? A courtesan. It's a profession as old as time.

I don't want to think about Dominic anymore. I need to take action, to feel like I'm the one in control again. In the upper right-hand corner of the website, I click a button that says APPLY. I can always change my mind later if it doesn't feel right.

Taking a deep breath, I start filling out the on-line form. I just don't know whether to pray for acceptance or rejection by the mysterious Allure.

● ● ●

The next morning, I fold up my blankets and then settle back on the couch with a cup of coffee and my laptop. An email from Allure has appeared in my in-box overnight. My heart rate jumps a little just at the sight of it. I hesitate, then click to open it.

The message is short:

Dear Presley,

I would like to meet for a brief interview. Would this morning at ten work for you?

Thank you,

Gia

Underneath is an automated signature listing her title as OWNER.

I check the time and suppress a loud curse. Thank God I naturally wake up early. I only have an hour to get ready and make it to an interview across town.

I've just clicked reply to let Gia know I'll be there when the front door opens. I startle and whirl around like I've been caught doing something illegal—which isn't far from the truth.

Jesus, calm down, it's just Bianca. You know, the person who actually lives here?

"Man, I'm so glad to see you." Bianca sighs as she shrugs out of her coat and hangs it up. "You've been working so much lately. You want to get something to eat and watch bad reality TV with me?" Then she pauses, taking in my wild expression. "Are you okay?"

Not at all. "Everything's fine. Just, uh, I gotta do some work stuff this morning." That's not a complete lie. After all, escorting might be my new job from now on. "But I can hang out later if you want?"

Bianca appraises me and then gives me a slow nod. "Sure. That sounds good."

I shower at warp speed, hesitate for a minute about clothes before yanking on the same suit I wore for my Aspen interview, skip breakfast, and then pray for the bus to be on time all the way there.

Allure's offices are in a totally normal-looking office tower. The décor is bland and the elevator plays soft jazz music. *What did you expect, a drunken orgy?* I chide myself.

At the fifth floor, a receptionist waits behind a sleek, polished white desk. She flashes me a smile that doesn't quite reach her eyes. "Good morning. How can I help you?"

Suddenly, I feel young and inexperienced, and completely unsure about what I'm doing here. I almost consider turning around and returning to the safety of the elevator. Instead, I straighten my shoulders and take a deep breath.

"Hi. I'm Presley . . . um, I have an appointment with Gia at ten?"

"Ah, yes, Miss Harper." She stands up. "Right this way. Would you like coffee or tea?"

"N-no, that's okay, but thank you for offering."

I follow her down the burgundy-carpeted hall to an oak door that wouldn't look out of place in Aspen's offices. She knocks, waits for the occupant to call out, "Come in," and opens the door.

If I'd thought the receptionist was glamorous, the woman standing by the window is astonishing. Gia is tall, statuesque, without a single, dark hair out of place. Her designer dress and heels probably cost more than my first car. I would guess that she's in her forties at the oldest, but maybe she's had work done. She clearly has the money for it.

Gia looks me up and down, blatantly assessing my appearance, then smiles and gestures to the leather chair in front of her desk. "Please have a seat."

Trying not to be intimidated and failing badly, I obey. The door clicks shut as the receptionist exits.

Gia sits behind her desk, her hands folded neatly in her lap. "Your application said you have a bachelor's degree. From where did you graduate?"

I force myself to stop wringing my hands. *Breathe, Presley. This is just another job interview. You know how to do those.* "Brown University."

"What field did you study?" Gia asks.

"I majored in economics." I start to relax a little at how ordinary this is.

"And what are your goals regarding your career?"

With barely a pause between questions, Gia interrogates me on everything I mentioned on my application, plus a few things she must have searched the Internet for.

Finally, she asks, "Why did you apply to Allure?"

My mouth dries up. "Uh, I thought, because . . .

I work hard, I'm a quick learner, and . . ."

Gia laughs for the first time. "You're allowed to say *money*, dear. Pretty much every girl in this industry has the same reason. People have expenses. Sometimes their life circumstances don't permit more conventional employment, and it's not crass to admit that."

"Oh. Well, then . . . yes, it's money. I'm supporting my brother through college, and my internship is—" *Probably shot straight to hell.* "—unpaid, but it's also full-time, so I haven't been able to find a second job that works around those hours."

"You weren't lying when you said you were a hard worker." Before I can figure out how to take that, Gia changes topics. "I want to assure you that nothing sexual will happen on these 'dates'. Escorts aren't slaves; I sell the company of attractive, interesting women, not the right to their bodies. Although you should keep in mind that the happier clients are, the more generous their tips will be." She smiles demurely while I try to read between the lines. "I won't guarantee that a client will never, ever try anything inappropriate, but you can report them to me, and they'll be banned from Allure. Now, are you still interested?"

Sex will definitely not be happening if I have anything to say about it. But maybe I really can do this. It'll be an extra grand in my bank account just for making conversation with some lonely rich dude for a few hours.

Slowly I reply, "I think so."

"Wonderful. I have the perfect starter client for you, an older gentleman who's requested a dinner companion for seven o'clock."

I almost choke. "As in *tonight*? S-so soon?"

"If you're busy, I can put you on our waiting list. Usually, work is assigned a few weeks in advance. This engagement is only available now because the original girl called in sick yesterday."

I lick my lips nervously and try to steady my breathing. She said all he wanted was someone to eat dinner with, right? There's no need to freak out—and no time like the present. I have to suck it up and jump in with both feet.

"No, I'll take it."

Gia smiles. "Perfect." Then she pulls out a folder emblazoned with the Allure logo and hands it to me. "Let's cover some details about what it means to be an escort."

I nod and then listen as she fills me in on the expectations of table manners, etiquette, and the art of making polite conversation. It's mostly common sense, but it's also a bit fascinating. I never imagined I'd be sitting here, listening to pointers like *never discuss politics or religion on a date, and how to appear amiable and interested, even when a client isn't at all your type.*

We spend another thirty minutes talking, and then Gia slides a piece of paper across the desk. "Here's the restaurant where you'll meet tonight's client. For safety, I'll never disclose your address or other personal information."

I take it, still feeling unsure, but trying to be brave. "Thank you. I won't let you down."

"I didn't anticipate you would," Gia replies with another of her small, enigmatic smiles. She rises smoothly to her feet. "Let me show you out."

• • •

Dale, the older gentleman I'm entertaining, is no gentleman at all. When I sit down at his table, the first thing he does is place his hand high up on my knee and give it a firm squeeze.

I blink at him and then shift in my seat so his roaming hands can no longer reach me.

He's almost completely bald, except for a few stray hairs above his ears. "You're beautiful, sweetheart."

"Um, thanks."

If my tone sounds flat, he doesn't seem to notice. He pushes a glass of red wine at me. "Ruth, right? That's my ex-wife's aunt's name. How old are you?"

Why am I not surprised to hear he's divorced? I'm already so glad I put down a pseudonym for Gia to give to customers. Instead of revealing any more personal details, I attempt to joke, "Don't worry. I'm old enough to drink."

"Never would've guessed." He leers. "You look downright illegal."

I sip my wine to clear the taste of bile out of my mouth. With no clue how to reply to that, I just repeat, "Thanks."

Luckily, he doesn't seem to care about my lack-luster responses. All through dinner, he keeps up a steady flow of degrading comments and attempts to touch my leg, my shoulder, anywhere he can get away with in a public place. If this guy's a "perfect starter client," I don't even want to try to imagine what an advanced-level client might be like.

As soon as the check hits our table, I jump up like a snake bit my butt. "It's been a wonderful evening, but I really should get going now."

Thank goodness Allure makes clients pay the base price in advance. Even if he gives me a crappy tip because I bailed so unceremoniously, I don't have to worry about getting totally stiffed. *So to speak*.

He frowns. "What's your hurry?"

I plaster on a saccharine smile. "I have to . . . take care of my mother. She's sick." Very sick. Dead for over a decade, in fact.

Before he can say anything else, I'm heading for the door. If I hurry, I can make the last bus home and won't have to drop twenty bucks on an Uber.

But he just follows me out into the parking lot.

"Let me at least give you a ride. It's dark out."

Like hell I'm getting into this creep's car or telling him where I live. "Oh. Um, thank you for offering, but I don't need one."

"Don't be like that. The night's just getting started." He flashes me a lecherous grin that practically drips slime. "Let's go someplace quiet where we can . . . talk."

My heart freezes. I open and close my mouth a few times before I manage to sputter out, "I d-didn't agree to that."

He heaves an irritable sigh, rolling his eyes. "Fine. We don't have to go anywhere."

Oh, thank God.

But panic skitters through me again when he reaches for his fly, muttering, "Right here works, too."

"What are you doing?" I yelp.

"The hell do you think, girlie? This is the part where you blow me." He starts to unzip.

I turn around and bolt so fast, my high heels almost trip me on the rough asphalt.

"Hey!" Dale starts after me, his face red and fly still undone. "Fuckin' bitch!"

I clatter across the street and between buildings I don't recognize. Someone honks—at me or him, I don't know. I just flee until I can't hear Dale's yelling anymore and it feels like there's a hot knife stuck in my side.

I flatten myself against a brick wall, my heart hammering, blood surging through my ears, and grip my side, where a cramp burns from my sudden sprint. My gulps for breath turn into sobs. I sink down, trying and failing to fight back tears. Needing a ride, I dig my phone out of my purse so I can call Bianca, a taxi, anyone. Even Dad would do at this point.

I tap the home button but the screen stays black. I scrub at my eyes and squint through the darkness. Did I hit the wrong thing? I try again, pressing the power button this time. Nothing happens.

Then I realize what's wrong, and a hysterical hiccup escapes me. Forget yesterday . . . *this* is the worst day of my life. And to top it all off, my fucking phone is dead.

Now that I'm not running in blind terror anymore, I notice the chilly air and the stale stink of the alleyway. Part of me wants to just sit here and hide, to make sure Dale didn't follow me. But I make myself stand up and keep walking.

I wander around, my feet aching, until I see the lighted sign of a twenty-four-hour gas station. I push open the door with a jingle and ask the teen-aged cashier, "Sorry, could I use your phone?"

"There's a pay phone outside," he drawls.

"I . . . don't have any change." I haven't carried cash since I was this kid's age.

He eyes me, then wordlessly takes the landline receiver off the wall and holds it out over the counter.

I've never been so grateful to look like a total mess. "Thank you so much."

He shrugs. "Yup."

Swallowing the lump in my throat, I dial the only number I know by heart.

Several seconds tick by, and the phone continues to ring. *It's an unknown number, he's not going to pick up*, I tell myself, fighting back another wave of tears. The cashier eyes me suspiciously while I attempt to wipe away the remnants of my mascara that I'm sure are on my cheeks.

Then a deep male voice answers, and its familiarity is almost as painful as it is reassuring. "Yes?"

"Dominic." I sob with relief. "Can you . . . please come get me?"

ALSO IN THIS SERIES

He's the powerful CEO. I'm the know-it-all intern.

Things went further than they should have, but I don't have any regrets. Well, maybe just one . . .

I went and did the one thing he told me not to—I fell in love with him.

Dominic Aspen is complicated, demanding, and difficult, and I want every ounce of this deliciously broken man. A man who fought to keep his twin daughters, who runs a billion-dollar empire, and has a hidden, tender side.

I have seven days to prove my trust and devotion. Turns out money is a powerful drug, but love is even more addictive.

Don't miss the stunningly sexy and heart-pounding conclusion to *The Two-Week Arrangement*.

Acknowledgements

I would like to thank you, dear sweet reader, for picking up a copy of this book. I hope you enjoyed it! I feel so blessed to dream up love stories for you to enjoy.

An immense thank you to my editing team of Elaine York and Rachel Brookes who were each so instrumental in helping shape this story. Thank you for loving Dominic and Presley!

I owe so much to my copyeditor Pam Berehulke. We are going on five years strong and I'm just so grateful for your diligence. You have taught me so much.

Thank you to my incredible assistant and right hand, Alyssa Garcia from Uplifting Designs and Marketing for your support and constant cheerfulness as we tackle well, all the things! A huge hug and a GIANT thank you!

To my sweet husband John for all the back rubs, the laughs and the sushi rolls over which we dream together. And thank you for never once rolling your eyes, no matter how cuckoo-bananas my ideas are. You're the reason I can do what I do. I am so blessed to have you.

Get Two Free Books

Sign up for my newsletter and I'll automatically send you two free books.

www.kendallryanbooks.com/newsletter

Follow Kendall

BookBub has a feature where you can follow me and get an alert when I release a book or put a title on sale. Sign up here to stay in the loop:

www.bookbub.com/authors/kendall-ryan

Website

www.kendallryanbooks.com

Facebook

www.facebook.com/kendallryanbooks

Twitter

www.twitter.com/kendallryan1

Instagram

www.instagram.com/kendallryan1

Newsletter

www.kendallryanbooks.com/newsletter

About the Author

A *New York Times*, *Wall Street Journal*, and *USA TODAY* bestselling author of more than two dozen titles, Kendall Ryan has sold over two million books, and her books have been translated into several languages in countries around the world. Her books have also appeared on the *New York Times* and *USA TODAY* bestseller list more than three dozen times. Kendall has been featured in publications such as *USA TODAY*, *Newsweek*, and *In Touch Magazine*. She lives in Texas with her husband and two sons.

To be notified of new releases or sales, join Kendall's private Mailing List.

www.kendallryanbooks.com/newsletter

Get even more of the inside scoop when you join Kendall's private Facebook group, Kendall's Kinky Cuties:

www.facebook.com/groups/kendallskinkycuties

Other Books by Kendall Ryan

Unravel Me
Filthy Beautiful Lies Series
The Room Mate
The Play Mate
The House Mate
The Impact of You
Screwed
The Fix Up
Dirty Little Secret
xo, Zach
Baby Daddy
Tempting Little Tease
Bro Code
Love Machine
Flirting with Forever
Dear Jane
Finding Alexei
Boyfriend for Hire
The Two Week Arrangement

For a complete list of Kendall's books, visit:

www.kendallryanbooks.com/all-books/